RIVAL TERRITORY

The Relic Recovery Series: Book Two

Dale Jefferies

A Book Quest Press Publication

DEDICATION

I must dedicate this book to my beautiful wife. Her patience and understanding is an inspiration, as-well-as a stimulation to the imagination.

CONTENTS

Relic (Noun)
1. An obsolete item of interest or sentiment, which survives from the distant past.
2. Common term/slang as defined in the *Gun Control Act* of 2073. Any set or series of impact based projectile weaponry that does not comply with the Gun Control Act, Pub. L. 722, which states (in summary), a projectile discharged from a firearm must identify the weapon's handler.

Snag (Noun)
1. An unanticipated obstacle.
2. Sample Deoxyribonucleic acid (DNA) Grappler.
3. Common term used to identify the mandatory feature in a legal firearm. Without a viable sample from the handler, a SdNAG module would render a weapon unable to fire.

CHAPTER 1 – FIVE AND SIX

The new weapons on the streets have given new life to an old ARRU adversary. Its name is "The Hidden Agenda." Deputy Director Karen Patterson, Bureau of Alcohol, Tobacco, Firearms and Explosives (2094)

"Yeah, Salvo, it should go without a hitch."

Steel was never a man known for small talk. I was surprised that he had even attempted it. Steel was a man of purpose, a man of mission. He was more a man of action, and if you were the type to constantly rehash your plans, you could expect to lose him. He wasn't going to be happy.

"Yes, well," I said, "I put in quite a bit of planning into this operation. I have a vision of how it plays out. The problem of mixing plans with visions is that visions are always perfect, but plans seldom are." I shook my head. "You and I know that nothing ever is."

I looked back at my life and reminisced on the days when I could've actually taken pleasure in what I was about to do. Those days were long-since-gone, but the darkness still had ties to the hands and the skill set was still there.

I ransacked my mind, trying to think of a better alternative. Yeah, there were some other options, but this one gave me the best chance of survival when – or if – the shit hit the fan and everything were to go belly-up.

I knew there were motion detectors surrounding the RV; the crew inside still made me go through the motions of knocking on the door.

I heard them scrambling about in the vehicle. I looked over at Steel and shook my head.

"Geez Christ," I said. "They're sitting pretty, all safe-and-sound in their Tank-Vee, with every kind of relic you could imagine, and it sounds like they're about to crap their pants in there."

Steel folded his arms and smiled. "If anyone should be panicking, it should be me. I've seen your amateur FFB friends packing some pretty lethal stuff. Most of the time, I don't know whether to dive or duck."

I gave the door another four good knocks, "Come on, it doesn't take that long to—"

The door made a small gust when it swung open.

Steel and I were greeted with the fire-making end of a relic-class revolver. On the other end was an old friend of mine.

"Salvo, you got some nerve creeping up on us at 10:45 at night," she said.

Steel dropped his head and laughed. "See what I mean? Duck or dodge."

"What's the matter with you, Chris?" I said. "We're here for the shipment."

She dropped the weapon to her side, but the roll of her eyes and smirk on her face told me that she could barely put up with the stupidity. "That's next week, you idiot."

Steel and I looked at each other.

"Are you sure?" I asked. "Are you telling me we drove all the way to Oklahoma for nothing?"

She turned her head and spoke over her shoulder, "Everybody stand down." She stepped back and moved back into the inside of the RV, leaving Steel and me at the door.

I stepped through the door and, as expected, we were surrounded: two on the left and two on the right.

"I hope you're a cat," a voice said.

I turned toward the speaker; one of the two on my left. He was trying to look as menacing as he could; I could see through the piece, it was all a bluff.

"Why is that?"

One side of his face formed a smile. "At least you have eight lives left."

I turned back to Christine. "Alright, just so it's not a wasted trip. What do you have?"

She shook her head, "We don't have anything. I mean... well... we've a lot of pieces and parts. I suppose we could throw together a quarter of the shipment."

I shrugged. "Okay, great. I'll take what I can get. So, about what time do you think we can get out of here? I'm supposed to be back at work in the morning." She looked at me like I was crazy.

She closed her eyes and shook her head. "We're not doing anything until in the morning. Even then, you're not going to get the goods until the end of the day. Nothing, I mean absolutely nothing, happens until the morning. For one thing, I need to contact the Commander to make sure it's okay. The product would be untested. We don't really want our product blowing up in our customers' faces."

"That's understandable," I said with a nod. "Hey, business is business. Alright, can you point us to the nearest motel?"

Everyone in the RV laughed at the notion I would be able to get one.

Christine pulled two blankets from a cupboard and threw them on the floor. "We start work pretty early around here. Be ready to go to work around 6:00 in the morning.

****

I woke in a sweat. It didn't matter where I slept; the bad dreams followed. I looked at the clock on the counter: it was ten after four.

I slipped from under the covers and reached over to nudge Steel. Before I could grab him, he turned and looked at me. If I didn't know better, I would've sworn he hadn't slept a wink. "I'm going to step outside for a breath of fresh air," I said.

He turned and threw the covers over his head at the same time.

I turned off the outside motion detectors and made my exit as quietly as I could.

I sat against the hood of the car looking at the stars. I was still a little groggy, so I slipped a strip of synthesized adrenal underneath my tongue. It didn't take long before the stars started to twinkle.

It was roughly twenty to twenty-five minutes before Steel came out to join me. I offered him a strip.

"No thanks, I'm good."

"So, what do you think?" I asked.

"I think we're on a tight schedule," he said, "and if we are going to do this we need to get started."

I nodded in agreement, popped the trunk, and pulled five bags.

Steel took a deep breath and slowly exhaled. "That wasn't part of the plan."

I gave him half a shrug. "Plans change."

Steel closed the trunk. "I see that I need to start sending out résumés."

Contractors. Basically, he was telling me that our contract was over when it was over. I was glad that I had prepaid 'til the end of the month. Best that money could buy; unfortunately, when you bought Steel, the money also bought his conscience as part of the package.

The sounds of the crickets were relaxing, and the fireflies dancing on the wind put me in a quiet place. It made what I had to do a little easier, but didn't take away any of the regret.

We put on our masks so the gas wouldn't overtake us. After we reentered the RV and accessed the sleeping compartment, I knew and took some comfort in the fact that the five-man crew wouldn't feel a thing. They were completely incapacitated from the canister Steel had set off after I had stepped outside.

The first bunk we came to was Christine's. I laid the bag on the floor. "You wanna give me a hand?"

"Well," Steel said. "Not really, but you're not paying me just because I'm good looking."

I had known Christine from way back. In fact, I used to go hunting with her father. I suppose those two reasons alone told me that I needed to set her in the bag gently.

Steel stood and stepped back.

I zipped the bag up to her waist, pulled up her shirt, and let my fingertips glide along the bumps of her ribcage, 1 – 2 – 3 – 4 – 5.

The black blade found the place between the fifth and sixth rib. Just in case, I covered her mouth, but the only sound was the wet noise of her heart being sliced in half.

I had sharpened the blade three times before we even began the trip. The truth was in how easily it slid to the hilt. It was like she hadn't felt the blade at all. She arched her back when the hilt slammed against her side and held it for about five seconds before she dropped back into the bag. It wasn't until after I removed the blade that I realized I had half an erection. I knew I was spiraling back down into that dark place. Damn it, I wasn't supposed to enjoy this; I wanted to somehow blame her for teasing me and arching her back like that.

I covered the slit in her side with tape to control the bleeding. Sure, the bags were leak-proof, but the tape was just another 'just in case.'

Steel helped me lower the next one down, but I guess he had his fill of the show. Once the guy was in the bag, he sat next to a window and lost himself in the world outside.

It wasn't until we got to the last bunk that we learned there were two people in the bed. This was a problem; there weren't supposed to be any kids in the RVs.

Steel grabbed the old lady lying in front of the girl by the back of the shirt and waistband and dropped her onto the floor. It was enough to bring her around to a semi-conscious state, but the drug kept her from fully regaining consciousness.

I put my foot on her chest and pinned her to the floorboard.

Steel shook his head, turned, and then reached for the girl hidden behind the old lady. Even though the girl was about ten years old, he picked her up and held her like she was a baby.

"Not going to happen," he said. The squint in his eyes told me that he meant what he said.

I heard the old lady mumble something; I put my index finger on her lips, "Shhh." I unfolded a bag next to her, raised her arms over her head, and then rolled her over onto it.

It didn't take long to find the spot between five and six to finish up. I stood, turned, and looked at Steel over my shoulder.

"Steel, the *only* way this plan will work is that there are no witnesses. I understand how you feel about it. You know it's gotta be done." I shrugged. "There are only five other people in the world that know the location of this vehicle. Its existence is only supposed to be the stuff of rumors. We can't take a chance on the knowledge it has been compromised getting out before we're ready. When the time comes, it could be our only refuge."

Steel let the girl's feet drop to the floor, put his arms under her armpits, and wrapped them around her chest. He held her up like she was standing and let her head rest against his chest, upright… facing me. With a free hand, he grabbed her by the chin. "Look at this face," he said. "Now listen to what I'm telling you. Not going to happen."

"Fine," I put away the blade. "So what do you suggest?"

"Hey, if nothing else, I'll chain her up in my basement until it's all over.

The caution in my face must have been obvious.

"Hey, fuck you!" he said. "No, I'm not thinking of trying out the pedophile thing. You, more than anyone else, should know better than that. You know how much I hate those bastards; but what you're suggesting is going a bit too far."

I noticed subtle movements in her face. "Mmm, Uncle… Uncle Salvo? What…eh?"

"Son of a gun; you know her!"

The words she managed to get out before she went back under took Steel by surprise. The look on his face was very rare for him. "Or, at the very least," he said, "she knows—or thinks she knows—you."

I tried to look as emotionless as possible. "You mean knew—I knew them all."

Whatever emotional moment he was having, he pulled it back inside and returned to being a hardened professional. "Okay," he said, "you drive the RV; she rides with me."

"What's your grand plan, Steel? We're going to be all over the place… at least four different states this month alone. You going to leave her chained up… lying in her own filth and starving to death in your basement?"

He reminded me again with that squint in his eyes. "Not going to happen."

I bent over and placed a piece of tape over the wound and zipped up the last bag. After I got in the driver's seat, I got ready to start up the vehicle.

"Wait a second," he said. He turned off the inside cabin lights, opened the door about two inches, and then put his ear to the crack. He listened for about ten seconds, and then looked over the park grounds for another ten before he left with the kid.

This kind of business I typically do alone, but I was kinda glad to have Steel along for the ride. There were not many I trusted, not to mention Steel's services were the best the money could buy.

Too bad about the girl, though. I'd always liked Little CeCe. The way I figured, we'd be back at the house by four. That meant I'd see her between five and six—or at least my blade would.

CHAPTER 2 – THEY'RE COMING

I'm a law-abiding citizen. I have a right—no, a need—to protect my family; but, I don't have a need to provide my personal genetic information for the government to do with whatever they want. I'll keep my DNA, if you don't mind.
Jerry Sandersaul, Chairman, Firearm Freedom Brigade (2074)

"Agrarian, it may take them a little time," he said, "but they'll get it together."

I gave Lenard a quick nod that I understood before he walked away. I understood, but I also knew that time was not on our side.

It was all now in jeopardy. We knew it would eventually be coming to this, so no big surprise. Yeah, they would come, and oddly enough, their coming was actually a necessity.

If we were ever to gain any ground, if we were ever going to set change into motion, our agenda required exposure. What better exposure than the Federal oppression machine. The people needed to know that there were still some in this new sanitized world with the courage to challenge those that would smother mother freedom.

The insider information gave us the heads-up on the date and time they had planned their assault. 'Eight days from now' is what he said. I looked at our clumsy attempts at the run-through of an emergency evacuation and wondered if eight would be enough.

Chaos! This group was definitely lacking in discipline. There was more shouting than what should've been action. This was supposed to be a simple operation, but from every direction, all I heard was the barking of orders, followed by a challenge and quite often the reference to a female dog and such.

We could survive the loss of several of our facilities; the loss of more than what would be considered several would certainly mean the demise of our organization. Any resemblance to a future after that meant shredding of what was left of our organization to the four corners of Hell and hiding underground in rag-tag groups with no structure whatsoever. Yeah, it was the promise of a dark, dismal future for those of us so lacking in discipline.

"Hey you…, you with the 'barber' malfunction, I'm talking to you."

The person that was testing me from behind was only three steps away from a rude awakening. I liked to think of myself as a fair man. The type of man, who would do anything for his people, and they had to know this.

As much as I had sacrificed; all that was at stake and it had come to this. I had to shake my head in disbelief that one of my own people would test me this way.

When the claw of his hand embraced my shoulder, the reaction was instantaneous. There were several actions, but in my mind I only perceived the counterattack as one single move. First I pinned the paw that he dared to place upon me to my shoulder. With a simultaneous spin and twist, my body became a drill, his arm became the bit. As I came out of the twist, my free hand connected with his throat. My eyes stayed focus on the target, but out of the corner of my eyes I saw his newly airborne feet before his rapid descent to the ground.

I spared him. Yes, I was a fair man. As I retained custody of his arm, he remained immobilized from the promise of pain. I gave him a moment, while he tried to regain some of the breath that had been forcibly extracted from his lungs. His mouth imitated the forming of words, but I only got gasps for air. I decided to give him a little more time to regain the ability to speak, so he could make his apologies that would be unacceptable.

"Agrarian, we need him. He's one of my team leaders." Lenard's voice was surprisingly calm for someone that was about to lose something of value. Coming from behind me, he appeared on my left and slowly stepped in front of me.

"Agrarian, give the guy a break," he said. "He may be a bit overly ambitious, but he is one of the guys that can get the job done."

The would-be team leader finally regained enough breath to speak in his own behalf.

"Sir, I didn't know it was you. I meant no disrespect. You have always been an inspiration to me."

How touching I thought. So I inspire and I was what the people aspire to be? I looked at him for a moment, and then returned a stern gaze to Lenard.

"Fine," I said. "I'll give him a break." The crack of his arm seemed a bit too much for everyone that was in an ear shot. With the exception of Lenard, everyone took one to two steps backward. Lenard simply dropped his head. He placed his hands on his hips, and then shook his head from side-to-side at the loss.

"I want everyone to listen and listen good. Every team leader, as well as every team member deserves his or her pound of respect. I don't wanna hear about another instance of another in this organization showing any other person an ounce of disrespect.

If you are a member of this clan, you will treat any and every other member of this clan as you would do me. Now with that little tidbit of information in mind, I want you all to go back to your stations, and let's see if we can't make this evacuation exercise a reality."

Everyone shuffled-off back to their station and jumped right into their role. Lenard pointed at an individual and motioned for him to come over.

"I'll need for you to take this guy over to the clinic." Lenard was very calm in his demeanor.

The guy on the ground said that I was what he aspired to be, it's obvious that he had heard my philosophies, but the real meaning behind them had eluded him. Lenard was there though. He was there in his actions and in his reactions. In him I saw the mirror of my own purpose. I saw the skills set and the focus that reminded me why I had chosen Lenard to be in charge of this facility. I saw discipline.

"We've already discussed this," he said. "We had a plan for the evac, but if you start taking out my key players, we shouldn't be surprised if the whole thing falls apart."

I held my hand up for a moment, and then waved the comment off.

"The team will and should learn how to function without key players, so now is as good a time as any to practice. In the coming days, I suspect we will lose many key players; however, the movement already has momentum and we can use that momentum to keep this organization alive.

Look, take a look around. No more arguing and everything is moving like clockwork. The evolution is now functioning as it should be, so I would have to say that the loss of this 'would be team leader' was not a catastrophe. In fact, this little incident has served a very useful purpose. It has motivated each of the units to operate as one cohesive unit."

One of his hands departed from a hip to scratch the new growth of hair on his cheek. The sound reminded me of sandpaper while he prepared his reply. He took a single step toward me and leaned in slightly.

"Still, you gave me charge of this facility; you should allow me to run it. This includes the handing out of discipline."

I gave a little nod, and then from behind me we heard the scream, 'Look out.' I turned to see one of our soldiers falling from a transport; unfortunately, the young soldier was on the bad side of a fifty-five gallon fuel drum.

I thought I had become totally desensitized to suffering, but the resulting crunch made even me a bit squeamish. As the barrel rolled away, it began to spill fuel on the ground. I knew I had changed considerably over recent years. The evidence was in the fact that everyone else ran to the aid of the soldier, but I only considered the possible repercussions of the fuel spill. My foot was enough to stop the slow roll of the barrel, but I would need some help to lift it upright.

"Lenard, I'll need a hand to lift this."

"I have a better idea," he said. "Roll the barrel until the fill cap is upright." He moved to take charge of the injured person.

I grabbed an on-looker and enlisted his aid in lifting the drum.

Lenard returned to where I was standing.

"The difference one man can make can be huge," he said. "There was a reason I had the man you sent to the clinic in charge of this area. We will survive this, but it will take time to repair it. Time we don't have."

The quiver of his left cheek amplified the level of irritation he had with me, but recent events and the promise of more to come left me numb inside. I had to stay focused on the mission at hand. His words, 'We shall survive this" clawed at my soul. If we were to truly survive, the sacrifices would be far greater.

"From this day forward, every life we take for our cause will be the knife sting of justice in the chest of oppression. Every life we lose will be a martyr, and the world will know that there are still some things that can't be bought or sold. Yes, there are still some things worth sacrificing everything for. That is the place where our movement will really gain momentum. Their commitment…, their enthusiasm will become viral and spread to every corner of the earth this I promise you.

Once the truth of our message touches the people that's when our fight really begins."

CHAPTER 3 – GO TIME

There will come a day when we look at each other and laugh over how silly we were to fight over a thing like relics: unfortunately, we will have to wait. When the day comes that we can laugh about relics, the whole idea that we even needed them in the first place would have long been extinct. Anthony Gray, Political Strategist (2085)

I made another final run through and checked my gear. I told myself that this time would be the last; I also knew I was kidding myself.

"Agent Harris?"

I had become lost in the mission at hand. I hadn't even noticed the Armory Team Lead watching me.

"Is everything okay there, Sir?" she asked.

"Hot, steady, and ready," I said. "Everything good with you, Weaver?"

"Well, I have to be honest with you. I'm only good with things that are moving. We need to get to 'Go Time' 'cause, like you, I'm gonna feel a little stressed until we get there. The good news is we're almost there." She gave me a pat on the shoulder before she moved to rejoin her crew.

Almost Go Time… Thank God, 'cause it had been a long time coming. The actual locations of the factories had only been discovered about five months ago but, up until the last month, it had been nuthin' but boring stakeouts and the monitoring of vehicles and electronic traffic.

The last two weeks had offered a little bit more excitement. The plan was simple. Over and over, we reviewed the plan and practiced the assault that would give us control of the replica relic manufacturing site—or, more to the point, sites—the three sites that had been discovered, two of which were located here in Texas.

A considerable amount of effort had been made to somehow keep the coordinated assault a secret. But, to be honest, considering the variety of departments and the number of operators on this mission, I would have been shocked if we somehow had managed to pull off that feat. There was way too much money and just too much testosterone in the air for someone in the mix to resist the urge to share information with someone that didn't have the need to know. Not to mention, the media had been buzzing our offices and using what you would call 'enhanced journalism techniques' to get the scoop.

My teams and I would have been more than happy to coordinate the operation and take control of the facilities here in Texas. That probably would have been a better route if they had really wanted a hush-hush operation. I knew that keeping all those wagging tongues under wraps would be next to impossible.

I felt we could take the facilities down one at a time, but all the big bosses had a theory that once we took the first one down—and considering our limited resources—the other factories would know someone would be coming for them next.

I tried to remain flexible, and it made sense. I could understand the concept and was willing to work with that. The only problem I had was the joint oper-frustration—at least that's what I called it. These were supposed to be some of the best operators in the world, but a guy like me wanted to know every little detail of the skill sets of the people he was working with.

There were people smarter than me who came to the conclusion that because the facilities to be raided also had people with ties to terrorist agendas, the FBI needed to be involved. Because they had illegal weapons, the ARRU should be involved; because they were trafficking internationally, Interpol also needed a piece. They were supposedly harboring prison escapees, so we also had ourselves a bona fide U.S. Marshall. Oh, and of course, this wasn't our town, so the locals needed to be here as a support element. I guess they could pose for the cameras once this was all over.

Seemed we had a representative from every major law enforcement agency here milling about in the darkness. I don't know how the Texas Rangers managed to get out of this one. I asked one of them how they managed it, and he said they were smarter than us. Maybe they were.

Yeah, almost Go Time. A huge amount of planning went into this assault. Go time: 4:15 am, fifteen minutes from now, and had to admit I was feeling a bit apprehensive. Everyone knew their roles. Everyone knew, except the people inside the facility, of course.

We didn't know for sure what types of weapons they had inside. The statisticians based their calculations of predictions and probabilities on the estimated damages caused by that damned G-Coalition a year ago and the types of weapons that had been seized and that had been seen floating around on the streets for the past year. With respect to the types of weapons that were inside, my gut told me something else.

I have had close encounters with the types of weapons that these types of characters held near and dear, and they were not the same types of weapons floating around on the streets. These guys were as serious as a cow-tossing tornado throwing a tantrum, and I knew that if we didn't take them by surprise, there would be no second chances.

"Paul, you ready for this?" I asked.

"About as ready as I'll ever be," he said, and then ran a check on his head gear. "Oh, and it could get pretty hairy in there, so keep your head down. And

No! I don't need one of your 'let's watch each other's back' speeches right now. If you keep your head down, your back will be horizontal. I won't need to watch it."

Paul seemed a bit on edge, which typically wasn't his style. I wrote it off as the same pre-op jitters that I had. Still, jitters or not, it was good to have at least one member of my team with me. I would have felt even more comfortable if Jay, Mercedes, or even the newest member of the team, Leslie, were here, but they had their own parts in the project.

Jay had the east, while central Texas belonged to Paul and me.

"You don't need to worry about me keeping my head down," I said. "If it gets ugly in there, I'll be down so low if I tried to move I'd be digging a ditch."

I saw an amber light from the forward station, which indicated the go time was in five minutes. We couldn't be sure of the type of tech they had inside, so radio silence was strictly enforced. The commands were only allowed to come from front to back by way of filtered lights. If I had objections or needed to voice a concern, I was out of luck. There was no way to let those on the front line know until the silence was broken.

Since the primary concern was the terrorist threat, the Bureau had charge of the entire operation and would be going in first. Fine by me—they had way more resources anyway. Paul and I, as well as the five armorers, were really only here for the relics and the capability to produce relics.

Go Time!

Two rollers quickly advanced across the field in silent mode, dragging behind them sifters to ensure that no booby traps lay in wait for the advancing tactical units—all this in spite of the weeks of aerial surveillance by both drone and satellite. Two tactical units followed closely behind, ready to split right and left once the facility was accessible.

The rollers blew the wall, and the units advanced. That was our cue. Once they went in, the communication devices were turned on, FIDs were synchronized, and the armorers advanced to provide tactical support to the primary units.

We quickly made our way across the field, now well-lit with hover support. I tried to focus on the chatter over the headset while we made our way into the facility. The FBI teams made their way from room to room, relaying "clear" as they secured any and all possible threats. That was their mission. Our mission was divided into two parts. One: provide backup support for the primary infiltration units; two: identify and secure the relics inventory and secure relic production capabilities. Since the chatter clearly identified that the Bureau guys had their end under control, we immediately moved to the second half of the mission.

"Paul, you guys watch your backs over there in the Red Sector." I tilted my head toward my team. "We're gonna take a stroll over to Blue."

"A stroll, huh?" Paul said. "You make it sound like a walk in the park."

"What can I say? I'm an optimist. Maybe I'll have the opportunity to stop and smell the flowers instead of gunpowder."

Paul smiled. "If you were a poet, that comment would make you an optimist, but from an ARRU perspective, that makes you a pessimist. You should *want* to smell powder; it means you've found the bad guys." He turned and gave the lead armorer a nod, and then they each tucked the butt of their tactical weapon into the pocket of their shoulder and moved into the darkness.

No time to waste. The Bureau guys were supposed to have the operational areas and sleep chambers in fifteen minutes. The initial path had been cleared, and we had thirty to secure the production and warehouse areas, and that included an initial search for any explosives or incendiary devices.

We moved quietly through the dark corridors to what the smart folks had identified and designated as Sector Blue. No explosives were expected, but every contingency had to be anticipated.

The intensity in the air made my skin tingle. I suspected that the combination of the intensity and the advancing in a crouched, close formation fueled the sweat that was beginning to flow over the top of my goggles and down the sides of my face. I thought perhaps it was the intensity, but I realized I was more focused 'on the ready' for some insane and slightly suicidal person to jump out of the shadows, hell bent on causing me pain.

The chatter over the headset seemed to slow as more and more areas were classified as locked down.

So far, everything seemed to be going as planned. The problem was that plans that ran without a hitch gave me a very uneasy feeling. None of my plans ever ran so smoothly. Any minute, the hammer was about to drop.

We approached the door that led to the Blue Sector. Everyone on the team took up safe positions at forty-five degree angles to the door. The lead armorer cycled through the visual settings of her eye shield. First, she checked for miniscule traces of electromagnetic radiation that could be emitted by a powered wire. Next, she reviewed the color spectrums around the door and looked for a non-powered one. Once we received the all-clear, the number two man positioned what we called our skeleton key in the seam of the door, and then turned to make sure we were all ready. He hit the key with the palm of his hand; this created a small flash of light and the key's laser sliced through the latch.

The agent in position two immediately kicked the door open, and we made a rapid insertion into the room. A quarter of the way in, everyone came to a complete stop. To our amazement, what should have been a room full of smoke-billowing, relic-producing equipment was completely empty. Even the word 'Clear' was followed by a subtle echo. You could smell it, though. Something had been here, and it hadn't been that long ago.

Fuel. Faint traces of fuel lingered in the air. If some uninvited guest like us came-a-knockin', were they planning on burning the place to the ground?

A single light glowed from the far end of the room. The individual illuminated by the light poured himself a cup of cocoa, better known as 'poor man's coffee.' He had to care that we were there, but he feigned total disinterest. Once he added a spoon of whipped cream, he moved over to a small table, sat, crossed his legs, and then reviewed some documents that lay in front of him.

The entire team took another hard look around the room, looked at each other, and then lowered their weapons. We slowly walked in the direction of the kitchenette.

It couldn't be this easy. Months of surveillance had identified this facility as one of the three major production facilities, and this one identified as the primary.

I had witnessed the recordings of smoke billowing from the roof that was positioned over this very room, yet I stood in a room bare from top to bottom. I quickly figured out that the rapid decline in the intensity of the headset chatter had a direct relationship to our current situation. The primary insertion teams ran into the same level of resistance that we had. In a nutshell, everyone had an altercation with diddly squat.

I shouldn't complain, but I had started to feel cheated. I supposed that it was better than chaos and screams of terror as we moved through the corridors. I wanted a 'win,' but what we got was a 'freebie.' At least it appeared as such, but these things must be taken with a grain of salt. Everything has some level of cost. Freebies can be misleading.

We slowly approached the kitchenette and, like some kind of choreographed dance group, we began to raise our weapons up to chest height at the same pace as our forward movement. We came to a halt shortly after breaking the entryway.

"Don't you move a muscle!" The lead armorer tried to make it sound like it was a do-or-die request.

The individual in the kitchenette paid no mind to the order. He continued to ignore the team, and apart from the occasional 'tink' of the china cup against the saucer, no other sound existed in the room. Agent Weaver was about to repeat the command, but right after she led with an "I said, don't…" I stopped her by simply placing my hand on her shoulder.

I walked in front of the guy, and even though he raised his head enough to where I could see his face, it seemed like he was looking right through me. He raised his head for the purpose of taking another sip of his cocoa, not to greet me; anyway, the raising of his head did give me the opportunity to identify him. This was Lenard Anderson, the person we had already identified as the commander of this facility. He looked slightly different than the pictures we had on file. He was still dirty and grungy but now bearded; the knife scar under the left eye gave him away.

The easy way to let everyone in the coordinated assault know what we had was the chatter. I cycled through the menu of my goggles with the multipurpose button to the 'Identify Friend or Foe' mode and then gave the voice command, "Identify!" The computer replied, "Scanning!" The scan didn't take long. Only one second later, the computer followed with, "Identified! Lenard Anderson, warrant issue for the distribution of illegal weapons—class: All classes, non-compliance of Gun Control Act of 2073 and the transportation and distribution of hazardous materials. Warning, this individual is to be considered armed and dangerous. Do not attempt to capture alone."

Anderson finally broke his silence. "I think they give these computers way too much artificial intelligence," he said. "For example, as you can see, yours has the ability to exaggerate, and from the expression on your colleagues' faces, anything it says is accepted without question." He pointed a thumb at himself. "Look at me. I'm an old man and I'm about two or three years away from my doctor authorizing me a walk-aid enhancement certificate. Do I look dangerous to you?"

I felt that chill of caution again. I hadn't thought of him as dangerous until he said he wasn't. When the bad guys say something along those lines, pretty quick after that is when you can expect the fangs to come out. Maybe it was just the sweet smell of the cocoa. Maybe he was using it to get me to drop my guard.

I raised my weapon waist high again. "Lenard Anderson, you are under arrest."

The statement, for some reason left me with a feeling as empty as the room in which we stood. It was obvious that they had known we were coming weeks in advance. Everyone had thought we were coming to a banquet, but it was apparent we would be leaving with a biscuit. A moment of distraction caused me to ponder his reasoning for staying behind, but only for a moment. It was more important that I stayed focused.

I motioned for two of the armorers to bind him. They moved in quickly, and I couldn't help myself, I just had to say it. "Hey, take it easy on him. After all, he is an old man."

The government considered these folks terrorists; he most likely considered himself a patriot. All I saw was a criminal that we had successfully apprehended without altercation or incident—nothing more, nothing less.

I didn't have to ask. The chatter over the headset said it all; he was the lone warrior in the facility. No other names bounced over the communication devices, and the Bureau guys had already sifted through most of the cracks and crevices.

The chatter was now focused on the celebration of the name "Lenard Anderson." They acted as if it was "mission accomplished." He wasn't on the ten most wanted, but he was on the FBI's watch list. Seems the ARRU had got the short end of the stick. Not a single relic found, nor the ability to produce relics on a mass scale that we expected.

Each armorer held an elbow as they walked him passed me. I expected a lie, but I had to ask, "Anderson, what did you do with all the equipment?"

The three of them stopped.

He closed his eyes, took a deep breath, and slowly exhaled. "This is a church; this is a place for sanctuary, for those fleeing oppression. So, when you ask what I did with all the equipment, I'm assuming you mean my bibles. Are you seeking the doctrine of my faith? All the answers are found in our bible, part of which is there, on the table.

I looked at the way he was dressed and couldn't help but inject a little more sarcasm, "Oh sure, all the clergy are sporting the latest fashion in camouflage gear these days."

I looked at the document and, just to be safe, scanned it with my goggles to ensure no small explosive charge was hidden between the pages or underneath. I picked it up, gave it a quick flip through the pages to make extra sure, and then dropped it into my evidence bag. "I guess I can expect to spend the next couple of weeks listening to the rantings and ravings of your manifesto, huh?"

"Bible—it's a doctrine of faith," he replied calmly.

"Oh, I see. You will have to forgive me. I guess I'm just having a hard time picturing you in prayer to the god of the bang-bang."

The look on his face displayed disinterest. It didn't make any difference if he didn't like my jokes, or whether my comment was cynical or sincere; my thoughts and opinions of his faith were of little interest to him. The feeling was mutual.

The two team members at each of his elbows shuffled him away toward the door. They handed him off to a team designated for the handling of extracted detainees. There were several of these teams because they had expected around seventeen personnel to be on location. The team that arrived for Anderson was very excited. I drew the conclusion that it wasn't because of the level of importance of the individual but because they had way too much time on their hands.

After the handoff, my team was once again freed up to resume their mission. Even in the dimly lit room I could see where equipment had once comfortably rested. The silhouettes outlined by the dust that remained were a dead giveaway. There were even more wheel tracks, which led me to believe that the equipment was moved around often.

The unanswered question started to haunt me: Where was the gun manufacturing equipment now? A couple of other lingering questions gnawed at me also. Where were the people that were supposed to be here—the operators of the equipment—and why was it Anderson who had chosen to stay behind?

The leader of the primary insertion team announced that the facility was secured. Yeah sure, secured in record time. Paul came over the comms and asked me to switch over to our secure channel.

"Hey Badger-One, can you meet me uptown?" he asked.

I switched over to our private channel and prepared for what I already knew he was about to tell me. "What you got for me, Coyote-One?"

"Sounds like you guys are hogging all the action over there," he replied. "The only thing I got for you is hopes and dreams; it looks like the relic replica operation is a bust on this end."

From the echo in the room where he was, I could tell his room was as empty as my own. The disappointment in his voice was amplified by the echo in his voice.

"Cheer up," I said. "It's not over yet. Yeah sure, they knew we were coming, and we should have seen that one. But, only two days ago, this place was billowing smoke with a purpose. They may have had a chance to pack up and pull chocks, but the stuff is heavy. They couldn't have hauled it very far. I suppose it's back to what we do best—investigating."

"I guess it beats ducking and dogging shrapnel, huh?" he replied.

A red dot started to flash in the corner of my goggles, followed by the words, "Incoming Transmission: Barnes, Jay: Are you free to talk?" I switched over to a secure encrypted line and inserted the ear piece. After I pressed the microphone against my throat, I knew it was okay to implement a secure conference call.

I took a few steps away from the insertion team for a little privacy, initiated a team conference, and then waited for the connections. The number of low audible beeps every time someone connected started to come in. Once I got the expected four beeps, I checked the identities. Five green dots showed on my goggle screen, and when I cycled through them, it identified each one of the guys. I focused a whisper to my throat device, "ARRU-7 online."

Jay was the first to speak, "Hey Boss-Man, I have to tell you, I could hang a 'vacancy' sign up in this joint. Hope you're having better luck over there."

I shook my head like he could see me. "Well, I can't say it was a complete waste of time. It's pretty much the same situation here, but at least we did put a thumb on Lenard Anderson, the so-called leader of this facility. The guy was just hanging around like he was the sacrificial lamb."

Jay gave a little laugh before he replied. "Same here. We got Melody Jenson, and so far, she's the only person we've found. They tell me she was in the kitchen beating up on a skillet of vegetable stir-fry. Her comment was, she got tired of waiting—the nerve of some folks."

I thought about it for a second. "Yeah, for a minute, I had the feeling that Anderson felt he was too old to run, but that's not the case, is it? These guys are always at least one step ahead of us, so everyone is going to need to keep it tight. They obviously know everything we are up to, but we have no idea—no clue whatsoever—what they're up to. I got a feeling that this is about a whole lot more than relics." I turned my attention to Leslie. "Leslie, I know I asked you to stay back and give Mercedes a hand with the interrogations, but it doesn't look like we are going to be sending that truck load of bad guys in your direction like we planned. We could use a hand over here."

"What about me?" Mercedes asked. I could detect a hint of why-her-and-not-me in her voice.

I came back with an answer that probably made her so mad that I know her butt cheeks tightened up hard enough to peel the skins off a bushel of almonds. "Jay, couldn't you use a hand? I think Jay could use some help where he's at."

"See, you're playing. I'm being serious," she said.

I heard a chuckle from Jay just before he voiced his objections to her comment. "What do you mean? Yeah I could use some help, and you know that you and I can do some damage."

"See, you guys are trying to be funny," she said. "That's a three hour drive, and everybody knows all the senior folks in town have taken all the vehicles. The only modes of transportation around here are the rollers, and three—almost four hours on a roller—well, let's just say I'd rather stick around here and wait for sloppy seconds with Lenard Anderson and Melody after the Bureau gets through with them."

The sound of Leslie laughing in the background for some reason lifted my spirits a bit after months of planning and such a crappy operation.

It was too late; I already had the image of the orgy in my head. "Agent Molina, you have a pretty gross way of putting things sometimes. Now I'll be stuck with that picture in my head for the rest of the day."

"Oh, you know what I mean. It wasn't meant to be sexual." I imagined a cynical eye roll from her when she pulled the phone away from her mouth to make a comment to Agent Baker. "See, it's like I told you, their minds are always in the gutter."

I smiled and nodded, "Well, you have to be careful. You know how impressionable young Jay is."

"Yeah, you know how susceptible I am to sexual in do indoors," Jay said.

Paul couldn't resist. "Don't you mean innuendos?"

"Nah, I had it right. I *do* indoors, mister smarty pants."

I felt we really needed to get back on track. "Agent Baker, you mind taking the almost two-and–a-half hour ride down here to Granger? Times-a-wasting, and I'm going to need to get back to work here soon."

"Piece of cake," she said. "A MARRV relief unit is heading that way in about ten minutes; I can catch a ride with them."

"That doesn't sound like a bad idea. Tell you what: have them hook up a trailer and bring two rollers down with you. There is 10,000 acres of feral hog and coyote country out here, and if we have to search the grounds, I'd rather not do it on foot."

"Got ya, boss."

"Don't 'Got ya' me; they're leaving in ten minutes, so you should be off the line—or at the very least, packing a bag and letting them know they have a rider."

Her "see you in a bit" was followed by the familiar double beep of the phone disconnect when she ended the call.

I looked over my right shoulder and attempted to gauge the level of frustration from the team. I got it. This phone call wasn't part of the plan, and we still had a job to do.

"Alright folks, let's wrap it up," I said. "We don't know what's going on up north yet, but let's lock it down, down here. I think we're in for a long day, so let's see just how much mileage we can get out of it."

CHAPTER 4 – IT'S JUST A THEORY

I'm not sure I understand this fight for relic freedom. It most certainly is not to make the world a better place. Barry J. Ericson, ARRU 2, Team Leader (2077)

Our search was a little slow due to the crappy level of lighting. The entire facility was set up to run by a number of generators. They hadn't left much; they'd even sucked the fuel reservoirs for the generators dry, so we had to make do with the night vision gear.

Even the solar panels topside were just for show. It looked like they'd moved any cells and everything required to make them anywhere near functional to another site a long time ago.

Someone suggested we use glow globes to light the way until we could get some natural gas on site. I had to quash that idea because I knew the light from the globes would interfere with the night vision gear.

Even though we had night vision, it still felt a bit awkward moving through the shadows. I could still see fairly well in the darkest areas; nevertheless, I kept getting that sinking feeling that there was some kind of evil hiding in the dark. Maybe it was just paranoia.

Paul and I worked our individual teams toward each other, but every turn and every corridor stopped short of giving us the access we needed to meet up. From his biometrics, I could tell that he was close. He was about fifty yards from me. The search had to shift from finding evidence to finding the location of a secret access panel that would let us get to where we needed to be.

While individual team members searched for a seam, a crack, or a would-be trigger that wouldn't blow our heads off and allow us access, I had the lead armorer use her tools to check for minuscule spectral changes in color, as well as heat signatures that could indicate a seam in the wall. Nothing.

"Alright," I said. "At the risk of destroying evidence, let's go ahead and cut an access through the wall."

The lead armorer drilled a hole and used an eyeball-camera to get a heads-up on what was on the other side.

"Looks like just another empty room," she said. Sure, another large empty room, but what was with all the secrecy?

The armorer with the skeleton key then modified and adjusted the key's mode from explosive cut to continuous burn and started to make his own personal doorway. With a few seconds remaining in the cut, a second team member took clamps to the newly created makeshift door and held it in place until everyone was in their proper position for the insertion.

"Okay, everybody, watch your step. Let's not lose any toes on this one."

The night vision mode of the tactical goggles pierced through the blanket of darkness. Biometrics gave us a heads-up that there were zero people inside. But biometrics couldn't tell us if there were booby traps; so, once again, it was one of those heel-to-toe situations where the heel that hit the ground was laid very gently.

We made it inside about ten feet before the whiteout hit. The room lights came on, and the glare of the overhead lights cause our night vision to go blind for a second. I guessed that someone had filled the generators and taken the liberty of firing them up to make our search less troublesome.

Damned sloppy is what it was. Neither Paul nor I had given the 'all clear' that there weren't any explosive devices present. That would have been a perfect set-up to tie 'shredders' into the electrical system. Maybe they figured we wouldn't be so incompetent as to fire up the lights without checking, so they didn't bother. Lucky us.

We all were well aware of the effect that bright lights had on night vision. I refused to wait for the goggles to make the adjustment. I ripped them off to find myself in what was without a doubt a loading dock. It didn't take much to find your boundaries in the place.

"I think I've found the door," I announced.

The wall lever that I flipped engaged a pulley system that started the descent of a ramp. The morning light that filled the room made all the trouble of turning on the artificial lights an afterthought. We had seen trucks come and go, but they never stayed for long, or so we thought. My first thought was that they pulled the old switch-a-roo with the trucks during satellite surveillance gaps.

I tried to get ahold of Paul. "Coyote-One, you and your crew wanna come and join us?"

I heard a short crackle over the headset, and then, "Still trying to find an entrance."

"Well, you got two choices: you can make one, like we did, or you can use the one topside." The short pause that followed was an indication of confusion or bewilderment. I wasn't sure, so I decided to elaborate. "I found a lever that lowered a vehicle ramp from ground level into the room."

"Oh," he said. "So how did you know it wasn't a booby trap?"

"'Cause the sign under the lever says 'Main Door,' but I don't see any warning labels." I heard a short chuckle.

"And you were worried about me doing something stupid? We'll be around and down in a minute."

It took them about five minutes to, like he stated, 'make it around,' but the 'down' was a delay by an FBI team they met up with at the ramp. Even though it was a pretty big room, I could tell it was about to get really crowded in here, real quick.

"Agent Harris," the FBI team leader spoke while he made his descent, "you weren't planning on keeping your assessments a secret, were you? I know you guys are famous, but I'd like you hear the opinions of a true-to-life hero also, if you don't mind."

I didn't know the agent's name, but his attitude was like that of so many others that I had met, so I decided to call him Sam.

"Sam, I reckon the only thing that hero stuff will get you—besides shiny little pieces of metal for your chest—is dead. If you're interested in joining the ranks of the heroes, I would recommend taking up needlepoint instead. You don't need to go find the big case; the big case will find you. The only thing you'll need is a plan, as well as a well-organized and a well-trained team. The rest will take care of itself."

Paul threw his hands in the air and looked over at the agent. "Geez, I told you not to get him started."

The agent and several members of his team produced soft laughs. "So what does 'Sam' stand for anyway? Smart-ass muther?" the agent asked.

I thought about it for a moment and considered the idea, but chose to roll right into assessments. "Arial surveillance has captured images of transports in the courtyard above. We've seen the transports enter the courtyard, loaded up, and unloaded. We've also seen them depart the yard with what we had always perceived to be a full shipment. What we haven't seen are their actual manufacturing operations in this place, which I suspect has always been a ruse." It was hard to tell if the expressions on their faces were that of contempt or confusion.

"Think about it," I continued. "Every transport that we've pulled surprise inspections at various weight stations throughout the country has yielded nothing— no evidence whatsoever. The transports that we've had under surveillance were all props. In fact, I'm going to go out on a limb and say this whole facility is a prop, but the actual targets of interest were kept— or better yet, temporarily staged—in this very room. Folks, I think we're looking for a type of transport that we haven't seen before."

The disbelief showed in the faces of the FBI agents, but everyone attached to the ARRU waited patiently for more info. I waited for one of the Bureau guys to shoot my theory down. It didn't take long.

"We've had this place under surveillance for the past three months," one of them said. "We've seen each and every transport that has passed through here. We have the makes and the model numbers; we even have the VIN numbers of the vehicles, so excuse me if I say your assessment has a few holes in it."

It wasn't their team leader that spoke. Seemed he knew as well as I did that someone on his team would put that question out there. He was smart enough to let someone else put their ass out there in the wind, just in case I could prove my theory. That way, he wouldn't need to worry about making himself look like an idiot.

"You're right," I said. "After all, it's just a theory, but some things you just can't get around. If you're fabricating a barrel, you'll have to shave, file, and bore it. If you're manufacturing on a large scale, it doesn't matter what level of obsession-compulsion for cleaning you have—you wouldn't be able to get all the stuff off the ground. When you walk on it, some will get ground into the floor. The dust will cover the wall, and as a general rule, the lubrication from the machinery tends to piss all over everything. There is no evidence of any of that here, so all we have right now are theories."

"With respect to the relics," I added, "I can't tell you where they're being manufactured, but what I can tell you is that they weren't being manufactured here."

The contempt showed in the young Bureau agent's face at my little insights.

"Agent Harris, could I have a word with you?" the Bureau team leader asked, as if he needed to assert his authority or position.

We took a short stroll over to one side of the room for a little bit more privacy. Not exactly sure why, because even with a quick look around, it was obvious the acoustics in the room would make it like an auditorium.

"Listen," he said. "It's what you guys do, so I'm going to leave the ball in your court with regard to relics and relic-related issues. But, I still have the burden of responsibility for this operation. You guys go ahead and see what you can dig up, but keep me updated on anything you find." He tapped on the communication piece on his headset. "Falcon-One."

"Yeah," I said matter-of-factly. "Responsibility is a pain in the ass."

He just smiled, nodded, and turned to walk away.

It wasn't important, but I had to ask. "By the way, how come you guys get really cool names like Falcon and Eagle?"

He stopped and looked over his shoulder. "I guess because we're on top—you know, flying overhead—whereas, you guys got the tasks of digging down here in the dirt." He smiled and then continued walking.

Yeah, right.

Paul appeared on my right side and gave a little shrug before he spoke. "So what do you think?"

The question seemed to magically create all kinds of scenarios in my head, based on historical and past experiences in joint operations. "Like the old saying goes, 'Keep your friends close, and give your enemies closure,' if you know what I mean."

"Isn't that, 'Keep your friends close, and keep your enemies closer'? You and that dang Jay are wearing me out."

"Well, I did say if you know what I mean."

He smiled and shook his head. "I guess you did."

I turned back toward the direction of the Bureau team. "If Falcon-One is afraid we'll steal his thunder, he's wasting a lot of valuable stress he could be using for something more important. Unfortunately, he is right about one thing. He has the charge of this operation, but if either of us were going to make any headway on this project, we are going to need to work together." I looked back at Paul. "Baker should be here in about an hour. We'll take the rollers and search the grounds, but I will need you to join the Bureau's Hover Crew and be our eye-in-the-sky. I have no doubt, and I'm sure they really want to work with us, but I'm getting the feeling that we need to add a touch of quality control to that effort."

CHAPTER 5 – THE SLOW AND STEADY

The truth is, no one really needs a relic. This is not the Wild West; hell, after you throw out the delusions and romantics, even the Wild West wasn't the Wild West.
Doctor Samantha Stapleton, noted Gun Control Advocate (2091)

The relief crew arrived about thirty minutes ahead of schedule. They must've been chugging along at a pretty good pace to make that kind of time.

I had to admit, I was glad to see them. We had already swept through the bowels of the facility three times, with nothing to show for it but frustration and disappointment. We needed to expand our search, and the grounds were as good a place to start as any.

I knew that Baker was working on her certs for interrogator, and it would have probably been best if she had stayed back and worked with Mercedes to clock a few hours on the OJT sheet. But I saw a little of myself in her—at least from my younger days—and I knew she was probably in need of some fresh air.

It was pretty obvious she was glad to be out of the shop. As soon as she opened the door on the MARRV, she threw herself out and planted both feet. The little cloud of dust that flew up from the landing gave me the impression she was ready for some action.

She put both hands on the back of her waist, made a deep backbend, and then, in three short leaps, she was past the vehicle and had jumped up onto the trailer.

I supposed it was rude of me to watch her strip down to her personales before she put on the spin-suit, but what the heck. She didn't care if anyone was watching, so why should I care that I did?

"Enjoying the show?" How dare Paul interrupt me during my moment. Yep, I was busted, but wasn't going to let it cause me any stress.

"As a matter of fact I was, or at least I was before being so rudely interrupted."

Paul crossed his arms across his chest, smiled, and leaned in." Did you get any pictures?"

"Please, I'm only just a bit of a perv, and that's going just a bit too far."

The contortions of his face let me know his disappointment. He used the top of his head to point. "I'm getting ready to hop a ride with the hover crew. Let me know when you two are rolling,"

I shook my head. "I'll let you know when we're riding," I said, with emphasis on the 'riding' part. "I don't do that rolling crap."

"Oh, this is the first time you'll be riding with Baker, huh?" He nodded and then turned toward the hover vehicle. "Let me know how it goes," he said over his shoulder. He covered his face with the inside of his arm and headed for the cloud of dust.

I turned back to see how it was going with Leslie, and then I realized the rumors may have had some truth to them. She hadn't bothered lowering the ramp, and you could barely hear the stealth engine when the roller became airborne and flew off the back of the trailer.

The four… well, more like two wheels—with the two front and two rear so close together—hit the ground and made a rooster tail out of the dirt. She zigzagged through people and equipment, scaring the crap out of a few agents in the process. Once she reached a clearing, I saw that she was picking up speed. I figured I needed to put a damper on her fun before she got too carried away.

I was a little annoyed that I had to put back on the bulky headgear to use the comms. "Alright, Leslie, this is the slow and steady. You're going to need to simmer down."

"Sorry," I heard over the headset. "Just doing diagnostics."

Both wheels locked up, and the vehicle slid at an angle before going into a single roll. I couldn't help but think what kind of brain thinks this stuff up. It was all by design. The usual road vehicle came standard with antilock brakes, but these—the brakes on the rollers were lock-only. Something about optimizing the kinetic energy of the slide and the roll. The only way to come to a slowed controlled stop was to use the lower gears.

The roller came out of the roll at a 90-degree angle from the direction of where the roll began. The tires created another fountain of dirt after they touched ground and she turned and then headed back in my direction.

Damn, it's great to be young. Unfortunately, the being young and thinking you're invulnerable has always been a dicey combination. Hopefully—if she doesn't get herself offed in the process—she'll have enough close calls on this team that she'll come to realize that this crap is a whole lot more than just 'look both ways when you cross the street.'

I heard the transmission shift into the lower gear, the training wheels extended, and the bike slowed before coming to a short sliding stop about four feet in front of me.

When her head popped up over the lip of the shell, it reminded me of the pictures I had seen in documentaries on the endangered prairie dogs. Maybe it was the skullcap of the spin-suit.

"Are you done?" I asked.

"I'm just getting started," she replied, with kind of a 'you better watch out for me' grin. "I love these bikes."

I thought about what she had just said: 'I love these bikes.' More like egg-shaped bathtubs would have been more accurate. But, they were very efficient as a tactical vehicle and, as far as tech goes, yeah, state of the art.

I knew she had disconnected the spin-suit from the roller once I heard it power down. With a brace of herself on the top lip opening and a hop, she was on the ground and was offering me a spin-suit of my own. I hadn't even noticed she was holding one when she got out. The form fitting nature of the suit was too much of a distraction. Too bad it wouldn't be as flattering on me.

I took the suit and decided to shift back into my 'mister asshole professional' role. "Don't you want me to update you on the situation?"

"You old guys, when are you going to give up the fight against change?" She closed her eyes, put her hands on her hips, and then shook her head. "Modern communications. I've heard and seen everything that has taken place from the time the communications blackout was lifted at entry into the facility, up until the pull into the parking lot. I saw it all on the monitor in the MARRV."

Yep, she was still in transition mode from armorer to investigator. She was still thinking and operating like an Armorer, but it was to be expected. After all, she had just only been assigned to us three weeks ago.

"Here's an idea: let's meet halfway. You keep all that knowledge you got from the live feed and most definitely use it. But, I feel that there is always something new to be learned from that human factor. A little face-to-face might reveal the fact that the person that did the search is really an idiot, and you might want to go back and take a second look. So, while you're on my team, you'll need to attend each and every face-to-face you get a chance to." The smile slowly faded from her face. "You are going to have to let go of that armorer mentality. You're an Investigator now, so go investigate."

She took a moment to remove the skullcap, used both hands to push back any loose strands of hair, and readjusted her ponytail. Half of that smile she had slowly returned, with a nod.

Her eyes suggested that she was working on the whole concept. "That makes sense," she said. "Hey, sorry— don't you worry. I'm a quick study, and I'll come up to speed in no time."

"Good, the red and blue teams are gathering for their respective situational updates, and since Paul is already in the sky, I'll need for you to sit in with the blue team, and I'll take the red. Remember, keep your eye on the ball, and we are always investigating."

"Gotcha," she said and shuffled off in the direction of the blue team.

Yeah, she needed to work on her interrogator certs, but I'm really glad I got her out of the cave. It was at that point that I realized that our ability to get things done was not because of any special training, equipment, or tactics. It was mostly because of our ability to get the information we needed, and this was in the old tradition of pounding the ground and beating the bushes. I also realized—even though they always gave me a lot of flak about them—that my little speeches were more of a benefit to me than to the team.

****

She didn't know that she was gonna have to go through one more briefing. For the last thirty minutes we had been moving from one debrief to another, and the whole time she was just a-fidgeting and a-twitching with anticipation to get back into that mobile bathtub she called a roller.

By the time I put on my spin-suit, she was already strapped in, doing more diagnostics, I guessed. I climbed over the top of mine and lowered myself in. I can't deny that the lower I got, the more second thoughts I had about doing this. As soon as my butt hit the seat, two lights, positioned slightly in front of my shoulders lit up the lower half of the roller and the communications system came on.

I didn't even get a chance to strap in and connect before I got a, 'Ready when you are,' over the speakers.

"I thought I told you to simmer down," I said.

"I'm just saying, you know, it doesn't take that long to lock yourself down. Are you okay? Would you like me to come over there and—"

"No, I'm fine thank you… just relax over there." I hoped she was trying to be funny. She couldn't be that twitchy.

I got the suit connected and the system came on. "Checking bio-records…" it said. "Welcome, Agent Harris. The high-velocity ensemble is indicating an elevated heart rate."

"Kyle…" I think Leslie was trying to push my buttons. "I'm getting a flashing yellow indicator on your biometrics. Are you sure you're okay?" Yes, she was definitely trying to be funny.

"Leslie!"

"Sorry," she said. "Just trying to help."

"Fine, just give me a second." I did my best to come up with some type of excuse that wouldn't sound lame. "You know what? This bathtub kind of reminds me of an elevator, that's all." I took a deep breath and slowly exhaled. "I have a problem with elevators."

"Alright, that looks a lot better." The kind of elevated, giddy tone in her voice let me know that her display suggested that I wasn't heading for a heart attack, which was a good thing because the suit came fully equipped with a defibrillation system.

"Alright," I said and made preparation to give a final briefing. "Let's do this. We'll start with sector 7." Leslie's roller took off and was already up to fifty-five kilometers per hour before I could finish my brief or even engage the throttle. "Leslie, what happened to the slow and steady?"

"Oh, but you know that at anything less than twenty-five 'K' per hour, these things run in low power mode. Just trying to save as much battery power as possible for the search."

Dang it, she was right. My planned 'slow and steady' included a ground search, which ran at about fifteen 'K' per hour. That would limit our search time to about half an hour before we would need to either hook up to a battery source or take to the open road to recharge the cells. The rollers could still use the alternative fuel for propulsion, but we wouldn't be able to use the scanners and onboard computers for ground hunt-and-probe mode.

"Right behind you." Crap, now it was either rethink the plan or get out and walk. A foot search of 10,000 acres in the hottest part of the day was never part of the plan. When my roller hit twenty-five kilometers per hour and the interior of the shell lit up and rendered a perfect 360 view of the terrain, it made the decision a lot easier.

Even though 'Hunt and Probe' supported speeds between ten and forty kilometers per hour, we still needed to be going at least twenty-five to charge the cells. Our search would need to be a little bit faster than fifteen. I really wanted to have the ability to have to roll the vehicle out of the equation, but I figured, *Oh well, so I lose my stomach once or twice and blow a few chunks.*

The roller hit fifty-five. I heard the gyros kick in, and then felt the turn-on of the gravity stabilizers in the shell. It felt like the suit began to tug on me from every direction until it seemed like I was floating in the middle of the shell, and then I realized, this was what Leslie called diagnostics. I got it. It was beautiful. The perfect 3-D image of the outside that was rendered on the interior shell, together with the floating feeling, gave a sensation of flying.

"Right turn," came over the comms.

Leslie hit her brakes and went into a forty-five degree slide. I was going to hit her; I was definitely going to hit her. I reacted as quickly as I could, hitting my brakes and going into a slide. The only option was a roll. I jammed the steering system hard right to make it roll. I knew that the hard right, in combination with a dip of my left shoulder, told the computer and gyro systems to allow a roll. Both our bikes made a single roll simultaneously. When we came out of the roll, we were side by side, heading in a 90 degree angle to the right of our previous direction.

The first thought that came into my head after coming out of the roll was, *The first thing I gotta do after I get out of this tub is kick her straight and directly in her ass.*

"Leslie, I just wanted you to be aware that I am going to kick you square and directly in your ass," I said, and then I heard what I believed to be a controlled laugh over the comms. Yeah, I'm kinda slow sometimes. It finally dawned on me that the whole thing had been planned and she was just playing. I had been pretty sure that all the things I heard about her had to be exaggerations, but I'm gonna have to say that everything that I had heard now had a little bit more sugar in the water.

"Oh, relax," she said. "Even if you were as crappy a rider that everyone has made you out to be and hit me, the worst you could have done would've been to send me into a double roll. I doubt that I would have even felt it."

Her brakes locked again and her roller slowed and fell behind me like she had thrown out a parachute. I wondered what kind of trick she was getting ready to play on the old man this time, but the distance between us had grown so that whatever she was up to, it wouldn't cause me much stress—I hoped.

I brought my roller to a stop as well. "What are you up to, Agent Baker?"

"We're on the edge of Sector 7; switching over to the slow and steady, boss," she responded.

"Oh, you just think you're so smart, huh?" I heard another low snicker that was meant to be under the radar. What a sharp kid.

I had pulled all kinds of strings and called in several favors that I was saving for a rainy day to get her on the team, but I would say it was worth it. Change was good, and the team needed some new blood. She was certainly a breath of spice and had no problem getting rid of the typical every day, mundane tasks that could cause the team to become burnt out. If nothing else, Mercedes would have someone she could shape and mold into her own image. Now that I thought about it, the whole idea of Mercedes shaping and molding was a scary thought.

The benefits were mutual, though. She needed the team as much as the team needed her. Life with the Investigators was damned hazardous, but she would have the opportunity to learn from the very best the Relic Recovery Units had to offer.

I thought about all the possible challenges that waited for her in the future. Now for my first challenge. *How do I get her to sit her ass still for five minutes and give her this last briefing?*

CHAPTER 6 – TARGETING SYSTEMS ON

DEMP (noun)
1. Direct Electro-Magnetic Pulse Generator.
2. Common acronym for a specialized weapons system, authorized for use by military, federal, and state law enforcement personnel. DEMP simulates a transient electromagnetic burst, concentrated into a controlled narrow beam. International law forbids the use of DEMP against personnel; however, it may be used against electronic weapons systems, vehicles, and other inanimate/non-organic life.

I had to change the plan. Sure, we could do the slow and steady, but the need to charge the cells every thirty minutes would put a serious kink in the amount of progress we could actually make.

I bumped it up to thirty 'K' per hour to make sure the batteries kept a decent charge. Of course, this wasn't enough to power up the interior shell, so to see, it was still necessary to either pop your head over the top of the shell, or wear the bulky eye interface goggles, which simulated the whole experience. I tried the goggles, but after the first hour the poor resolution was starting to give me a headache.

I chose to stick with the real deal and poked my head over the top, as well as use the hunt-and-probe interface.

The lip of the shell fell just below my shoulders, but it wasn't too bad; unfortunately, the reflective skin of the outer shell made it a whole hell of a lot hotter. Not to mention, at thirty 'K,' I had to stay really focused because there was a chance I could miss something.

I hated it, but now I was really relying—no, dependent— on the tech. I had read about some of the miraculous things the ground scanners could find and do. It was kind of a big leap for an old Investigator like me, who was used to pounding the ground and eyeballing everything, but I had a backup. Paul, working with a Bureau Hover crew, was shadowing us, and they had a whole lot of tools I had a lot of faith in and was familiar with.

The explosion came from the south. I just knew that what had started out as an enjoyable little distraction had been shattered by something that was about to ruin my day.

Central Operations took over the comms. "HC3 is down; I say again, HC3 is down!" I put back on the interface to get more info. "All available units, converge on the site and render assistance."

I looked to my left and saw HC3 on the ground, flashing shades of red. I touched the 3-D image, and from the pop-up menu I selected status. The screen came back with a long system functions labeled as 'inoperable,' followed by biometrics. Two of the three-man crew were still alive.

"Ready to go?" Leslie asked. I figured she could catch up, so I just hit it.

It didn't take long to reach a speed were I got that sensation of flying again. All systems were on and now feeding me new and updated information. HC3 was four kilometers away. HC1—which Paul had chosen—was behind, but would soon overtake us.

A small window appeared just to the right side of my face. It was the feed from a drone that had just come into the zone. HC3 was on the ground, but you could only see the mangled front and rear parts of the aircraft; the rest was hidden behind black billowing smoke.

"Are you getting all of this, Kyle?" You could almost feel the intensity of the anger in Paul's voice when HC1 zoomed past us.

They had to have known this question was coming, so I asked, "Yeah, any idea what happened?

"Telemetry information is coming in now," he said.

Text from the drone flashed three times and then locked: Relic class, 20mm.

History appeared and slowly started to scroll up the screen, outlining the details and the weapon's class, followed by an "Oh shit" from Leslie. I had to agree.

These types of weapons were developed in World War II to bring down aircraft. They later found that they were damned efficient at busting up tanks. With that being the case, one thing was for certain: I didn't want it pointed in my direction.

Even though there was a 20mm in the equation, the bio readings from one of the survivors were getting weaker, and I didn't know how long he could hold out. I really, really wanted to keep my distance until we got a decent assessment of the area; but, the 'officer down' wouldn't allow that option. We had to go in.

The hover crew Paul was with must've had some kind of chunky guts. They made several circles over the downed craft, knowing full well that there was a relic somewhere out there that could chew them up. I just knew they were about to become a six pack of buns and wieners sitting next to a fat man in a carnival hot-dog-eating contest.

"Kyle, you two need to stay back. We're checking the area."

A faint, unrecognizable voice came over the comms. "We were getting some minor thermal signature readings from underground. About half a kilometer to the north. Watch yourself." I realized it was one of the two survivors of the downed crew.

"Take it easy," I said. "We're coming in to get you."

"You two need to stay back." The tone of Paul's voice was enough to throw the roller back into low gear. "HC2 is almost here. We can provide air cover while they drop a team and evac them out. We don't need any more people to rescue."

Since I had no desire to become a statistic, I decided to go with the plan.

I could see on my screens two drones hovering in the danger zone that the downed crewman had identified. Telemetry information started to come in and then stopped. The two pop-up screens from the drones turned into white noise. Three seconds later, I heard two explosions, followed by what was undoubtedly the sound of two very expensive drones slamming into the ground.

I popped my head out of the top of the shell to see two columns of smoke in the distance.

"Alright Paul," I said. "You guys help out HC3. We are going into the red zone."

"Are you sure you don't want to wait for backup?" For some reason, the caution in Paul's voice made me want to go even more.

"Jeez Christ, you sound like a little girl," I said. "What? You getting all cranky 'cause your training bra is riding up on you? Tell you what, you just hang out and hover, while the grown folks handle this."

"Well then, you go right ahead and get yourself a 20 MM enema." Any air of caution in his voice was now gone.

"You ready, Leslie?" I asked.

"Could I have just a second to adjust my trainer?" she responded.

Yep, I had a real joker on my hands. "No, you can't. So whatever you got, they're just gonna have to dangle."

The whistle of the engines started a low scream as we raced off into the direction of a very bad day.

We were coming up on the zone pretty fast when I realized that I didn't really have a plan. I was allowing my personal agenda to run me. I had to get a grip.

"Leslie, we're going way too fast for a 'Hunt and Probe,' so let's do a quick circle and grab an image. You go right and I'll take the left."

"Woohoo!" Her excitement was starting to make me a little nervous. She was having way too much fun with this. "I'll grab position 1," she said and then sped up.

She pulled in front of me, and I tolerated her dust while the imaging systems synced up. Once the on-board computer came back with "Position 1 – Locked," she immediately went into a slide and a roll. It was like déjà vu, and I was right back in the same situation I had been with her before, but, this time I couldn't slow the roller enough and my roller bumped hers. It sent her into a second roll before I went into my own. She went right, I went left, and the muffled laughter over the comms was a reminder that, yep, I definitely needed to kick her directly in her ass.

I watched the 3-D image render itself between our two rollers. Yeah, it was way nicer than having to compile the image set. First, it grew as a line and shot straight up as we grew further apart and then got wider when we turned to make the circle.

"Alright, we know we're not alone out here, so keep it tight," I said.

"Hey, got the booty cheeks clamped onto the seat and ready to roll." She had a flair for creating visualizations, and that was one I could work with.

We were heading straight for each other and about to close the circle. "Les, since you have position 1, you take the inside." I just had to make sure that we didn't hit head on. I didn't care how tough these bikes were, that would be a very, very bad thing. The only response I got was another 'woohoo,' which was seriously poking at my 'nervous' button.

She still passed close enough to cause my screens to white out on me. She was right about one thing, though. The miniature earthquake she created inside the shell from the pass made my butt cheeks grab ahold of that seat and flex like they belonged to a body builder.

My screens came back online and a complete image of the circle we had just made showed up as complete. Yeah, fast rendering, but unlike the regular image set, this one came up only as a green display. Could have been better, but readable.

We were making our way back around to the original location where we began the circle, and I made preparations for another Agent Baker fly-by. I still had another quarter of the circle to go, and she was already at the starting point.

To my amazement, she came to—what could be considered—a normal fish-tailed sliding stop. No roll, nothing fancy, just a stop. Made me wanna shout 'woohoo.'

"Leslie, you're out in the open. Let's take up position behind that ridge at your four o'clock." Her roller disappeared in the cloud of dust from the doughnut she made to the left. I wanted to criticize her maneuvers; after all, wasn't that the long way around to a four o'clock?

At first, I thought she was just showing off, but then I realized that she was using centrifugal force as well as the weight, balance, power, and gyro systems to make that thing break the limitations outlined in the specs. I had to face it: the girl could defy gravity and could make the roller dance. I decided to shut the hell up and pay attention. Maybe I could learn something.

Since we didn't know where the 20 was hiding, we took cover on the side of the ridge. I knew a roller could handle small arms fire no problem. *Let's see, what does the manual say? Oh, no ill effects are suffered from devices that expel fragmentations and supersonic rapid expansion of gases.* I thought it would have been a whole lot easier if they had just said you could shoot the damned thing with a RPG. I guess people who write those manuals have to 'toot' their own horns sometimes.

The system continued to feed information into the image we had just taken. I watched as more and more detail built on top of the image.

"I guess if there was something that stood out for you, you would have said something by now," I said.

"Nothing yet," she replied. "Maybe we are looking in the wrong spot. Did we tag the right zone?"

"This is it, but what did the HC3 pilot say? Ah, computer, display ground thermal readings." The system beeped and the 3-D image flattened and rotated to an aerial view. "They were getting temperatures anomalies in the terrain. Alright, as hot as it is, my guess is we should be looking closely at the dark areas."

"Yeah," she said, and I felt a touch of confusion in her voice. "Well, if they are underground, then there's a fake tree out there and they're tangled up in a web of roots. Those are the only cool spots I see."

"Uh huh," I knew we were close. "But, we know somebody or something is a-creeping out here, so let's keep looking." Over the low hum of my systems, I heard what I believed to be the start of another engine.

"Agent Harris?"

"What are you doing over there, Les? I'm not in the mood for another 'woohoo,' you hear me?"

I felt the overpowering urge to pop my head out of the top of the shell, so I did but very, very slowly. The new engine sound was coming from behind the ridge, which rustled slightly in the warm breeze.

"I swear," she replied. "I haven't touched a thing."

Then I heard two short revs of an engine. "Uh oh," I said. The side of the ridge flapped like a flag in the breeze. "Then I think you better touch something real quick and hang on to it for dear life because—"

I thought this is what a bowling pin must feel like when the vehicle that burst through the phony canvas ridge sent us both bouncing in opposite directions.

After I finally stopped bouncing, my roller laid on its side, spinning in a circle, and then immediately stopped. The spinning wasn't very agreeable to my stomach, but it must have driven the system's gyros nuts. The low speed stabilizers had dug into the ground and stopped the spinning and had already started to lift the roller upright.

Leslie didn't wait for her bike to become upright, though. As soon as the stabilizers had lifted her about forty-five degrees, her wheels were on the ground with enough traction to go into her doughnuts. It was beginning to make more sense now. Get the wheels spinning, which powered up the generators, which in turn brought all those power-hungry systems back online. My turn.

I hit the throttle and leaned in to start my doughnut. Absolutely beautiful. Two-hundred degrees later, I was bringing the bike out of the circle directly in the direction of the vehicle that was making a break for it; unfortunately, the momentum coming out of the turn threw me into another roll. Positively pitiful.

The sound of Leslie's voice over the comms made me grit my teeth because I knew whatever lame excuse I came up with, she would see right through it.

"Are you okay?" Her roller started to slow.

"I… huh, I think one of my gyros might be damaged."

"Oh sure. Do you need—"

I wasn't about to let her rub it in. "Shut up and go get 'em."

I saw the speed counters go up when her bike sped off in the direction of the RV. When the stabilizers started to lift me again, I decided to let them lift me to enough of an angle that wouldn't bruise my ego.

I got about a good sixty degrees before I made a pretty impressive fish tail and I spun off in the direction of the chase. Finally, something to brag about.

Leslie was almost on them. After all, how fast could a mobile home go? Well, okay, actually, a modified mini-mobile home.

I knew it had to be coming: The "Oh shit" that I didn't want to happen. The sleeping giant had awoken. The 20 rose out of the top of the mobile home, sitting on a rotating turret. Not your typical RV out on a weekend excursion. This was a Battleship, and it looked like they were prepped and ready for war.

The gunner was trying to get a lock on Leslie, but she was too close. He couldn't train the weapon downward enough to get a lock on her. Even if he could, he would have to shoot through his own vehicle to hit her. The weapon was housed in the center of the vehicle, so she was alright as long as she stayed close enough behind.

It was obvious that they had set up for an anticipated aerial attack, so they set up an anti-aircraft relic, but I think it dawned on both the gunner and myself at the same time that I was far enough down the road and at a very nice firing angle. *Well, just damn it all to hell.*

"Leslie, I'm going to need you to take out the gunner on the top of the vehicle. If you don't, I swear I'm going to haunt your body." I was looking down the barrel of a 20 at a thousand meters. "Leslie? I think—"

A single round created a miniature crater just to the right of my front wheel. A miss, but still enough to cause my roller to swerve off the trail and through some brush.

At first, I thought he might be using some type of grenades the way the ground had exploded, but the bike's systems identified it as a 20mm projectile. Now that's a big bullet. The worst part was, I was sure that the single round was for targeting. Now he was adjusting his sights. I was sure that what would come next would be full auto.

At the same time I hopped back onto the trail, HC1 made a fly-by and covered me in dust. I was not sure if they were trying to offer me some type of cover or were just in a hurry to catch up with the oversized RV. Either way, I'd take what I could get. The 20 couldn't get a lock on Leslie, but I could see sparks flying off the shell from a heavy amount of small arms fire coming from the rear end of the vehicle.

I was again impressed by the tech. If I looked over the lip, I couldn't see a thing for all the dirt and dust, but on the inside skin of the shell it looked like just another beautiful sunny day.

I saw the barrel of the 20 tilt upward toward HC1, but the advanced targeting system of the hovercraft already had a bead on him. One round, a single round from HC1, tore through the gunner's chest. The shot caused him to bend over backward and then slowly fall forward. His head rested against the butt-end of the 20, causing it to tilt almost straight up and down.

The threat now gone, here was my chance to catch up. I punched it, but Paul put an end to that.

There was a crackling over the comms, followed by, "Kyle, we're going to need you and Leslie to drop back a quarter of a klick. The DEMP is fully charged, and we are going to hit them in 8…, 7…, 6—"

Dust flew from Leslie's tires. She held down on the brakes until I caught up with her.

I could tell the Direct Electro Magnetic Pulse generator was about to fire because the whine of the weapon sounded like a woman screaming. The flash that followed reminded me of the old cameras that needed a burst of light to capture an image. I saw the front end of the vehicle dip and the tires of the RV bounce, but it didn't even slow down. The burst should have fried every electrical component in the engine. The wires should have gotten hot enough to melt the insulation, but it was obvious: they were very well prepared.

"Shielding, they've got shielding!" I couldn't tell if Paul was mad or surprised. "We're detecting a Faraday cage around the whole vehicle."

It would take at least five minutes to charge up the DEMP again. They didn't have the time.

A woman popped out and onto the turret, pulled the first gunner inside the skin of the RV, and then released full auto on HC1. The hover crew apparently didn't have time to enable the advanced tracking systems on her before she could start shooting, but I saw the opportunity to take her out.

"Targeting system on," a see-through grid displayed in front of me. "Auto-tracking on," a red-circled, cross-haired targeting symbol followed my right eye over the grid. With a wink, I had a lock on her. "Release!" The computer came back with a "Please select type of weapon." Damned tech. I guess there are some advantages to having no tech and a relic. The only bad part about tech is you have to be smart enough to use it.

A single round flew from Leslie's roller—a miss. The round hit the receiver of the 20. Didn't do any damage to the weapon, but it was enough to scare the crap out of the new gunner and force her to take cover inside the skin of the RV. The damage had been done, though. HC1 was leaving a trail of smoke that had a nasty angle pointed at the ground. The trail of smoke was a zip line to what was luckily a level area that gave the ship a nice bounce, or maybe I should say skip, since it reminded me of a rock bouncing across the surface of a pond.

"It's your call, boss. Do we go after the runners or check on the crew?"

Leslie's question was a no brainer for me. "Since you managed to get the handler of the 20 to duck and cover, I think we need to close the gap on them before they re-man the weapon." I knew that without the type of air cover that HC1 could provide, we would all be toast if that happened. "We are just going to have to pray they're—"

I looked to my left and saw Paul staggering from the wreckage. The signals I got from him weren't 'Save me,' they were 'Go get 'em' and 'don't let them get away.'

Both of our engines screamed, and the gap was closed in no time. Just in time, too. Lady gunner was back on top, but we were already inside the firing angle of the 20.

Small arms fire pelted us from two inch slits made in the rear of the vehicle. The relic classes they had chosen weren't a stressor. The rollers could handle classes up to 7.62mm and standard fragmentation grenades easily. The problem was we were headed for the south gate, and there was nothing on the other side of that gate but a bunch of civilians that wouldn't appreciate us going Wild West on the town.

"Les, we need to stop them before they hit the town. You have any ideas?"

"Oh, shoot," she said. "We don't need ideas; we have tech. All you had to do is ask." If I'd had a free hand, her comment would have had me scratching my head. "Computer," she continued. "Display and select disabling target vulnerabilities." A new screen popped up and began scrolling text. After about three seconds, it started to pause intermittently, even though the volume of information was the same. Finally, it displayed a live feed of the RV, with a callout of selected vulnerabilities shadowed in green.

"Is that it?" I asked. "What about the tires?" A pop-up appeared and flashed in red. It identified the tires as reinforced carbon nano-tubular polymer, military grade. Basically, it was telling me that I would stand a better chance of putting a bullet through the Rock of Gibraltar.

According to the display, it appeared that our best hopes at stopping this vehicle would be to put a very lucky round through one of the tiny slits in the sides of the RV they had made to drop small arms fire.

"Alright, we are running out of time," I said. "I'd call in another HC, but if their primary weapon—the DEMP—can't make a dent, all we would have when they show up is another crew to rescue."

"I think I might have an idea." Leslie's comment added a little more pressure on an already tense situation. And here I was thinking that these kids today just allow the tech to do the thinking for them.

Leslie's roller sped up and took up a position to the right and about a quarter from the front of the vehicle.

"What the hell are you doing?!" I shouted. "You're too close. They can lay fire down into the top of your roller. They're on you… they're on you!"

Her bike swung hard right, which was an even bigger mistake. Now she was in the firing angle of the 20. I jammed on the brakes so I could drop back and get a clean shot on Lady Gunner, who had once again reared her ugly head and mounted the 20, but even harder than she had swung right, Leslie swung back to the left and jammed the roller between the rear wheels of the cab and what I'd call the trailer-part of the RV.

The RV's forward momentum sucked in her roller and rose higher and higher as the shell of her vehicle rolled underneath, going deeper toward the center of the RV.

The backbone of the RV finally snapped in the middle, where the rear of the vehicle used her roller like a lever. The middle of the vehicle that had been lifted in the air dropped down into the dirt, and the RV ground to a slow stop; fortunately, her beaten and battered roller impersonated a zit of a teenager when it squirted out of the rear of the vehicle, after the RV finally came to a sliding halt.

Her roller lay on its side, spinning in a circle. The system screens linked to her bike all showed the words 'Communications Failure' on top of a white background.

I didn't have her on comms anymore, so I pulled alongside and came to a sliding stop to see if I would need a spatula or a sponge to get her out of there. I didn't have bios anymore, but the exterior view on the inner side of the shell worked just fine. Every time the bike's top opening spun around, I looked inside and saw her waving her fist and—I had to guess—mouthing the word 'woohoo.'

The rate of spin slowed, and I saw her release her security straps. She finally brought the bike's spin to a stop by putting her hand out of the opening, dragging it in the dirt. She slithered out of the roller's carcass, stood up, dusted herself off, and then admired her work with a hands-on-her-hips attitude and a big smile.

"I'm just so freakin' amazed that worked," she said.

"I'm absolutely amazed you're such a freakin' maniac," I added.

Les bent down to see if she could salvage her vehicle.

"Oh you can just forget about it." I think of myself as an optimist, but I was already sure that was a lost cause.

Automatic fire from the rear of the RV started bouncing rounds off the shell near my head. It's a good thing they went for me first. It gave Leslie a chance to take cover behind my roller.

"Stay with me; use my roller for cover." I started to move to a slightly elevated position: A position that would give us the most tactical advantage until we got some bigger guns on the scene.

"I can't see the main weapon," she said, with obvious concern about my movements and the 20. "Let me know if someone makes a move for it."

The outside terrain was so well defined on the interior skin of the shell that I still felt the need to duck and dodge the sparks, even though I knew that I was safe inside the roller. Unfortunately, I was moving away from the RV, and the primary battery of weapons on the roller were forward facing. I attempted to keep an eye over my shoulder and watch the 20, but I also had to keep an eye on Les, who was walking sideways with snag drawn just off the nose of my roller.

I made it over to what I thought was the best possible position and turned and selected the disabling target vulnerabilities feature. One of the assailants was down, and the computer was counting gunfire from four access points, as well as the thermal signatures from a total of five individuals inside the RV.

I had to ransack my mind, back to what little bit of roller training I had on the weapons system, to see if I could bring this thing to a close.

"Target, vulnerabilities, and human signatures. Select 9MM, fire for effect. Release." The weapon's fire was very rapid and sounded automatic. I knew that there wasn't one on board, but the release was so fast it sounded like a Gatling gun. I saw the thermal silhouettes behind the weapon access points simultaneously drop to the floor of the RV.

One of the remaining silhouettes moved franticly back and forth from one end of the RV to the other. I targeted a single access point and waited for the person to pass behind it one more time, but the assailant started an ascent to the top of the vehicle instead. It was Lady Gunner.

She stood on top of the RV with her arms outstretched. I didn't know if she was trying to form the shape of a cross or if she was giving herself up. Since she had a weapon in both hands, I went with the cross, and she was only seconds away from martyrdom.

"I got her," Leslie said and moved from the cover of my roller.

"Where the hell are you going?" I was beginning to think the kid had a death wish. "Leslie!"

"I got her… I got her," she said. "Look, Lady, whatever you're thinking, whatever mistake you're planning, I have to tell you that you don't have to pile a big ole giant one on top of a bunch of little ones. I'm talking about the bad choices and the mistakes we all make in life. All your friends are down, but you're still breathing. That has got to count for something. Your friends are no longer able to tell their story, but you can. You can tell their story, as well as your own. You can make us all understand. Whatever it is you're thinking, whatever else is left is just another mistake. Come on, Lady; help me help you. What do you say?"

What did Baker see standing there in front of her? Was it hope? Was it the chance to rescue some misguided soul that had been led or wondered onto the wrong path? What I saw was commitment. The grimace and distorted expression in her face told me that there was no hope of changing the determination of her resolve. Then I realized I hadn't seen two weapons in her hands before. True, in her right hand she held a relic, handgun class, but in the left was the trigger of a detonator.

I finally got it right. I got my wheels spinning, made a perfect half doughnut, and dropped the bike in front of Baker, close enough to grab and pull her in head first. I just ignored the pain of the head butt I got in my crotch and tried to get as much as I could of her in the shell.

The explosion sent us on three bouncing rolls. The roller's power was gone, and with all the dust and dirt floating around in the shell, we were blind and could barely breathe. The dust started to slowly clear, but I could only make out the flashing red lights, letting me know that all systems were down.

Little by little, I was able to make out more and more detail, such as the spin-suit covered left buttock of a brand new agent that was starting to test my nerves.

"Get out, Baker! Get the fuck out!"

She backed out of the opening and tried to help me release my connections and restraints.

"Get your damned hands off me!" Crap, I was trying to make her feel guilty or at least think about the downside of what could have happened, but she simply just started laughing. "Alright, giggles, you wanna cover us just in case a badass machete momma comes running out of the flames with an attitude?"

She climbed back in and clambered over me to reach her snag that was leaning against the floorboard. I wondered if she'd put her knee in the side of my neck on purpose on her way back out.

I could see her little spin-suit boots standing outside the opening of the roller. I thought, *Boy, if only I had a hammer...*

"All clear," she said. "I don't think nobody is going to come running out of there."

I unhinged myself and climbed out of the mangled remains of what used to be my transportation. The first thing to hit me was the heat coming off the slowly liquefying RV.

I turned to see it entirely engulfed in one big giant blue flame. The RV was a bomb. Not one for causing casualties and mindless destruction; they simply wanted to destroy the evidence we could use against their group.

The grimace of Lady Gunner said a lot to me about her resolve, but the charred body parts scattered over the landscape told a completely different story. It was good to know who you were dealing with, and their story didn't start with 'Once upon a time.' It was more like 'You'll never take me alive.'

"Oh shit, Leslie, take a look over here."

"What?"

I was once again very impressed by her. She made a very nice tuck when she rolled down the side of the hill. She sat there in shock for moment before she tore into me.

"What the hell was that for?" she asked.

I hadn't kicked her directly in her ass, but the sole of my foot against her ass cheek and a good push was just as effective.

CHAPTER 7 – WRATH OF GOD STUFF

Yes, the technology is impressive, but you will never be able to convince me that a government salivating on the idea of complete control of its people has those people's best interests at heart. Agrarian Mann, Professor of Law, NYU (2089)

I was really surprised at how easily and without challenge I could walk into the field-office of the ATF. I had better security on my outhouse. Most expect their enemies to try and sneak in through a side window, or come calling by way of the back door. I suppose not many expect him to turn the handle on the front door and walk right in. Amazing that they've survived this long. I had heard that this crew was one of—if not the—best.

The chaos of their joint operation was my advantage. So many new faces, and mine was just another one of them. I counted three groups: the regulars assigned to this office, the out-of-towners (who were mostly the ATF brass that came down to monitor the operations), and the Bureau guys.

It was hard not to laugh at the fact that I could just walk around among these guys with half my wallet hanging out of my shirt pocket. You would have thought the scraggly beard would've given me away, but it looked like sleep was a rare commodity for these people, at least it had been for the last couple of days.

"May I help you, Sir?"

I stopped and slowly glanced over my shoulder with a smile, and then I realized that the receptionist wasn't even talking to me. Two of the out-of-towners were probably nagging her for a stapler.

Damn, I can't imagine who would decide to sacrifice such a sweet little old lady. When evil came, evil would not feel sorry for her. She would be the first to go.

Ah, target found. I had to guess she must've had a long day. I could only imagine the pace they've had her try to keep up with. I hated to wake her, but this was kind of important.

What a pretty girl she was. Maybe it was because she was napping. I found myself in admiration of the soft features and perfect skin. I imagined her, a dainty little thing that served the salons well. Could the rumors be true? A girl with highlights in her hair couldn't really be that tough. One thing was for certain: she made the women in my personal relationships look pretty ragged.

I expected her to jump up when her media device started ringing, but she didn't move. I continued to approach her, and she just sat there, leaned back, arms folded. It would be so easy to—

"What are you doing? And, who the hell are you?"

Nice. I found myself staring down the barrels of two nicely maintained Standard DNA Grappler 9mm standard ATF issue handguns. I hadn't even seen how she had pulled them.

"Do you sleep with those things under your armpits?" I asked.

No reply. The squint of her eyes said she was trying to read me. The tilt of her head suggested that what she read, she understood.

"Agrarian Mann."

I expected surprise, but she said it like she held me in contempt.

"Agent Molina, I'm pleased to finally meet you. It's my understanding that there were some questions you—well not you personally, but your people— wanted to ask me."

She looked left and right and then slowly lowered her government-owned Snag weapons underneath the desk. "Ay carajo, you got some balls to walk in here like that. And what's with that?" She pulled the weapon in her left hand from underneath the desk, and pointed at my wallet with the dangerous end before dropping it back underneath.

I smiled and said, "You know, you're actually the first person that noticed."

She looked around again.

"I'm curious," I said. "What type of concealment holsters do you carry? The draw was smooth and quick. Very impressive."

She brought the weapon in the right hand up, held it over the table, and then rotated it counterclockwise until the back of her hand faced up. She pulled her finger out of the trigger and pointed at me. "You want to smell my finger? Go ahead, smell my finger."

Yep, the rumors were true. She was as tough as they said, and since I was really turned on, I also came to the conclusion that I had been dating the wrong women. The standard had just been raised.

She made another quick look around, this time with a little stealth.

"You don't need to worry," I said. "I came alone, and there are no hordes of robot soldiers at the door with laser-guided relics mounted on their shoulders about to burst in."

Finally, a hint of a smile.

"Do I need these?" she asked, and then I heard the tap-tap of two side arms from underneath the table.

"I'm sure that you will someday. But, today? Not at this moment."

She paused and studied me again for a moment, and then she concealed her weapons again. One was kept—and it was my best guess—on the left rear hip, the other just below the inside of the front belt buckle, and from the contortions of her face, I had to seriously entertain the idea of smelling her finger.

"The Bureau has first dibs on every suspect bagged on this project, so as you can see, I've got a lot of time on my hands. I've spent the last several hours going over live feed or recordings of the interrogation of your friends Melody Jenson and Lenard Anderson." She used her forehead to point over my shoulder. "If they knew who you were, I have no doubt that they would come and snatch you up."

"Well," I said, "since you're a law-abiding government tool, aren't you going to turn me in?"

"Government tool," she repeated with a little smile. "I suppose I would, if there was a warrant for your arrest, but we put the word out that we only wanted you down here for questioning. You've managed to hide your tracks very well, Mister Mann."

I folded my arms across my chest and nodded. "Then I guess it's just me and you, Agent Molina of the legendary ARRU 7."

She had one of those stares that cut right through.

"So, how can I help you?" I asked.

"Well, first of all, why me?" she asked. "You could have turned yourself in to anyone in here. As a matter of fact, you didn't even have to come in this office, but you decided to prance your ass on in here and make your way straight over to my desk."

I wasn't sure how it would come across, but I had to laugh at her. "First of all, I don't prance, and this is about the infringement of freedom. This is not about anything the FBI wants. From what I've heard, my friends' primary mission is and has always been the reversal of the Gun Control Act. To raise awareness on the attacks of our liberties and the pursuit of happiness."

She made a slow shake of her head 'no.' "And you believe I can help you with that?"

"My friends—"

Her interruption was sharp and quick. "You can stop with the 'my friends' crap. Everyone knows you are the highest ranking official in the organization. What is it they call you... The Commander?"

I chose to ignore and continue because I knew time was short. "My friends, along with everyone else, see you as the face of oppression in this war for the freedom to bear arms. They felt that it was only appropriate that I deal with you... the ARRU, not the Bureau."

She threw her hands in the air, and then allowed them to fall back to the top of the desk. "Oh, please don't start. I've heard all the rhetoric." She pulled the weapon from her left hip and held it by the trigger guard and receiver. She held it firmly and laid it softly on the top of the desk. "The only difference between your weapons and mine is I take responsibility for my actions. When I put a bullet in somebody with this weapon, I basically say it's my bullet and I claim ownership of the events that have just taken place. That takes a considerable amount of courage." I noticed that the little light on the side of the weapon was now amber in color; unlike when she first drew her weapons.

Yes, she was very quick. Her eyes never broke away from my own, but she grabbed the handle of her weapon the same time mine was coming over the top of the desk. We both pushed our weapons forward at the same time; however, in the push forward of our weapons, mine ended with a click. By the time the amber light switched to green, I had placed my weapon on the top of the desk and was slowly raising my hands.

"Even though the technology is very impressive," I said, "your weapon has to get the sample and determine if the sample is viable. That is a considerable amount of work, and after all that, it still has to unlock, prepare, and run the firing train. Yes, the technology is very impressive, but the compromise you've made in the name of firearm freedom could someday make you dead."

I think I made my point, maybe too well. She held the weapon steady, aimed directly at my throat. Her eyes didn't show any anger, but her left cheek slowly started to tremble. Shortly thereafter, a very healthy vein started to bulge from the right side of her head. I had always been able to key on the eyes to see the next move. I had to admit, she had me dumfounded.

If the intensity of how hard she flipped the desk in my direction was an indication of how mad she was at me, she was pretty damned mad. I did manage to get my hands up and block the table with my forearms, but her foot on the underside of the desk still had enough force to tip me over and put me on my back.

The next thing I saw was that angelic face behind eyes of vengeance. She landed with both feet on the table, pinning me to the floor. The green lights from her two weapons could have passed for the pupils of her eyes; it made her look more demonic than angelic.

"Don't you fuckin' move," she ordered. "You lied to me. You told me that I didn't need these things."

The lady continued to amaze me. Most would have felt some sense of trauma, fear, or anger over what they believed to be the misfire of a relic in their face. It was obvious that she was only mad because I had lied to her.

I felt I needed to plead my case, but I was also sure the shouting of commands to drop her weapons and the people around us that had drawn theirs would somehow be a distraction. Still, I had to try. In our first two minutes, I had come to enjoy our little relationship.

"I can see that a man—or maybe men—has been lying to you for some time now and you don't appreciate it," I said. "I didn't lie to you, Agent Molina. The would-be weapon is a certified historical relic replica. I have the documents in my pocket to transport it. Signed, sealed, and certified." I patted the pocket for emphasis. "I don't know the guy that hurt you, but I want you to know that whatever animosity this person or persons has created in you, I'm just as mad as hell as you are for them having done so. A lady like you deserves so much more."

I wasn't sure if my attempt to bond worked or not. The expression on her face didn't change, but the trembling in her cheek stopped.

She wasn't a heavy girl, but I felt it when gravity brought her knees down to the top of the table. The weapon in her right hand found my right temple; the one in her left found a home in the pocket of my jawbone. Her new position was followed by a more intense volley of commands to drop the weapons and more attempts by the onlookers to gain some type of control of the situation.

She took a slow look left, and then right. Suddenly, she threw her hands in the air and grabbed both weapons by the trigger guard and receiver.

"Fine," she said. "But, I'm the interrogator. I don't like people trying to get inside my head, so stay out."

I saw the right shoulder drop, but the elbow was a blur. Just like everything else she did, it was quick and precise. I wouldn't be able to explain how or why I felt that sense of peace before the lights faded and I entered complete unconsciousness.

****

It took close to three hours—after I awoke chained to a hospital bed—to convince the FBI guys that I was more than happy to share any knowledge I had, but I would only do so with Agent Molina. They told me that she was on a temporary suspension, pending review. I told them that was a shame because that meant that they were temporarily shit out of luck.

It was okay, though. They didn't have anything on me, nothing that would stick anyway. At least, not until after the little fiasco with Agent Molina. The extra time allowed me to bring in my councilor, because now the Feds were pushing a threatening a Federal Agent agenda. Anything to get their man, right?

She entered the room without a knock and casually strolled over to the side of my bed and—I guess the best way to describe it was—threw those little fists on top of those hips.

"They're telling me that you want to talk to me," she said.

I ransacked my brain for something clever to say, but I could see that she was still a little on edge over the fact that I had lied to her. The best I could offer was the thing she wanted most: the truth.

"I see they removed your temporary suspension. I'm glad. I may not agree with the duties of the ARRU, but I would hate to think I was the cause of you losing something that was important to you."

She just looked at me. The single slow blink had to represent an 'I don't care' about my thoughts.

"Anyway," I continued, "the reason I asked for you is I believe without a doubt that you are a person of integrity and that even though you and I are on different sides, we are both fighting on the same frontline." Yeah, a little mushy, but it was the truth. I guess it kind of worked. The grimace from clinched teeth was gone, and all that stood in front of me was a mean a feisty, Tasmanian devil of a woman.

The truth was working, so I decided to continue. "We both have a serious problem, Agent Molina. No, I'm not asking for your help, but I am giving you a heads up. For some time now, there has been an ongoing type of civil war in the organization that you and your people have just assaulted."

"Don't you mean the criminal organization we are currently in the process of dismantling?"

I hoped that the smile I was trying to hold back wasn't interpreted as preparation for another lie. "I suppose it's a matter of perspective. In any case, the fraction that I share a common sentiment had hoped to resolve your unjust and illegal stranglehold on firearm freedom through a political and legal solution. The other fraction under the misguided leadership of—I'll put it this way—a rising star in the organization has high hopes of initializing change through much more radical means."

"Does this rising star have a name?"

"He calls himself Salvo, and unfortunately, I don't have the details of their agenda."

She crossed her arms, rolled her eyes, took a deep breath, and slowly exhaled. "Aw, come on, his momma couldn't have hated him that much to give him a name like Salvo. Could you give me a name that I can use?"

I gave her a simple head shake no. "The rule is, no matter whatever differences there may be in the organization, only secret names are used outside the group."

"Oh I see, like when they call you Commandante."

"That's Command—," I stalled my correction, but it wasn't until I noticed her chin and eyebrows raised in a new sense of awareness that I realized that she just got me to confess that I was that person. I had to smile; she remained stone faced.

"You think that you have caused irreparable damage to the organization," I said, "but that's far from the truth. This is a movement. This is not just some sandcastle you can kick down, or a person to kick while he's down. This is a religion, and Salvo believes his is the hand of God. I'm trying to impress upon you the seriousness of the situation. The bile that has been coming from Salvo's mouth is wrath of God stuff."

"Oh," she said. "I think I've been down this road before. If we take him out, we'd be doing you a favor."

"No, if you take him out, you would be doing the movement a favor, as well as yourself. My concepts and ideals are not a danger to you; however, there are some that hold the belief that it would be better to force the idea of firearm freedom by making it too costly to maintain the Gun Control Act." Finally, I noted a hint of worry in those eyes.

"How do we find this Salvo?" she asked.

"I wish I could tell you for sure. You could always follow my lead, I suppose; but unfortunately, every time I get close, I have to slow down to step over the trail of bodies."

CHAPTER 8 – IT'S A WASH

I personally will not rest until every single relic is destroyed. I will not rest, because the souls of those children slain by relics will not either. Jasper Clay, Director, Bureau of Alcohol, Tobacco, Firearms and Explosives (2082)

Alright, a brand new day, and I get to start it with a brand new set of bandages. The best thing about finally implementing the project yesterday is that all the extra sacks around here will soon be packing and heading back to wherever they came from.

"Good Morning, Edith," I said.

"Morning, Agent Harris." She squinted and gave my face a good look over. "Sorry, someone told me that you had lost your eyebrows in the raid yesterday."

I had an idea where that might have come from. "Did the person that mentioned that happen to be about five-eight, dark chocolate hair, and about one hundred and thirty-seven or so pounds? Oh, and wearing a shoe print on her backside?"

I didn't get a yes or no answer. She just covered her mouth with her finger tips and laughed. I really didn't think it was all that funny but had to laugh along with her.

She dropped her hand. "Well, whoever said it definitely exaggerated. You look as handsome as ever."

"Thanks, but you better cut it out. You know I'm dating someone."

She gave me a somewhat seductive smile behind aged but white teeth. "Oh, if I were just twenty years younger; better yet, if you were ten years older."

I couldn't hold back the laugh. "Don't you mean twenty years older?"

"Oh, please," she said. "I don't need an old man. I like mine young and tender."

Well, I figured that was enough for me. I gave her a wave, "Alright, likes them young and tender." I made my way over to the kitchen, grabbed a cup of cocoa from the vending machine, and then had a seat at my desk.

I figured, yeah, maybe come in a bit early and get my mind right for another one of those days. Since she is usually the first one here, I thought for sure I would see or bump into Mercedes, but I had even managed to beat her in—and then my phone rang. I looked at the identity and there it was, Agent Baker.

"Hey, you're not calling to tell me you're going to be late are you?"

What used to be a joyful little laugh now started to sound like an evil, plotting snicker. "Oh no, I was just wondering if you were still mad at me."

"Well, I was never really mad at you, it's just that—"

"Oh," she said, "okay I'll be right over."

I couldn't tell if her interruption was relief or excitement.

The click of the phone was followed by the sound of her chair sliding away from her desk from across the room. So much for the idea of 'come in a little early and take a little time to get my mind right.'

She plopped herself right down into the chair next to my desk, threw her right arm across her chest, and gave herself a good stretch by pushing on her elbow.

"Whew, what a day, huh?" she said. "Thought I'd come in a little early and catch up on some of the paperwork. I got the chase done, but I still need to give them a description of how to destroy a roller. When I went to requisition another one, I got a couple of dropped jaws after I had told them mine had been… well… rendered non-functional."

"Is that what you told them?"

Well, not exactly in those words."

I had to close my eyes and shake my head. I laid in, starting with my index finger, "Leslie if you have some kind of death wish—"

She threw her hands in the air. "I don't… I don't," she said, and then gently grabbed my hand with both of hers. As she was slowly pushing my hand down to the top of the desk, I couldn't help but notice how warm and soft her hands were. They almost made me forget why I had started laying into her in the first place. I started to think 'what kind of lotion?' instead of 'the nerve of some folks.'

She started to bat those eyelashes at me—as if it would make a difference—and continued. "It's just that… well, even though a lot of great things have changed for women in the office, a lot of things in the workplace are still the same. A woman still has to work twice as hard as a man just to get half the credit." It was like she was trying to impress the concept into my soul by squeezing my hand.

"Oh please," I said. "You act like you're suffering, but you're singing the sad song victims of Civil Rights have sung for well over a hundred years."

"What is this crap?" Mercedes appeared from out of nowhere over my right shoulder. The seriousness in her voice made us both pull our hands back away from each other.

"Dammit, Merce, what have I told you about sneaking up on me?" I demanded. "Do I need to put a bell on you or what?"

"Oh, don't let me interrupt," she said and then waved with one hand, about waist high. "Y'all don't have to stop holding hands on my account."

"Look," I said, "this is a counseling session, and a private one, if you don't mind."

The roll of her eyes and the wobble of her head made it hard to tell whether she believed that or not, but it didn't matter.

"Merce? This is private," I said again.

She looked at Leslie, but it was all a ruse. I almost wanted to laugh at the fake evil-eye she shot at Leslie, followed by a slow lean over to my ear.

"We need to talk," she said.

And there they were. Those infamous words women used when they needed to share their feelings. *We need to talk.* Oh dear Lord.

"Fine," I said, "but, you are going to have to wait your turn." I expected her to give me an eye-roll, but I got a hard double squint instead before she walked away.

The sneak attack by Mercedes caused Leslie to be a little on edge. She was sitting properly in the chair, hands in her lap like some little school girl.

I pushed away from the desk and drove my chair around to where she was sitting. "Look Leslie," I said, while grabbing her forearm, "I don't know what kind of baggage you're carrying, or what kind of relationships you had with the people you worked with before, but now that you're on this team, you need to push it under the bed. I have good news and bad news for you—it's all a matter of perspective— but no one on this team is ever going to treat you any different. In fact, if you screw up, I have no problem kicking you square and directly in your ass. On this team, you're just an Investigator, and I will only judge you on how well you can do the job. I expect the same from everyone else on the team, also. Well, except for Jay. You know he has had this crush on you since way back."

She dropped her head and laughed. When she picked her head back up to look at me, the Leslie that I was really starting to get to know was back. There they were: those movie star teeth, underneath a sinister but playful smile that gave you sort of a warm tingly feeling all over.

"You know," she said, "I don't want you to think I'm brown-nosing or anything like that, but even though everyone told me that I would have to put up with and endure your little miniature lectures, so far I have enjoyed every one of them. You just tickle me to no end."

It must've been one of her interrogator tricks. The smile that swept across my face probably could have lit up a room, and then for a moment… for only a moment, I entertained the idea of a swinging from the chandelier, hot sticky monkey sweat kind of sex affair with this one. Only for a moment though; I would never be able to get away with it.

"Yeah, it does sound like you got a big ole' hunk of smell good on your nose there and you can just give it up, 'cause you ain't gonna get a Christmas bonus."

We laughed for a moment and then stopped and looked over our shoulders toward Mercedes's desk. Mercedes just tilted her head and raised her eyebrows. We turned to each other and laughed again before Leslie got up and returned to her desk.

Both Jay and Paul came in together, Paul a little slower than usual. After that Hovercraft crash yesterday, I knew he had gone to the hospital to get checked out. When I called to check up on him and heard that he had been released, I figured it couldn't be serious, but there was obviously some pain there.

"Paul—"

"Don't worry, just some bruised ribs."

I guess he had already rehearsed it before he got in.

"Nothing broken," he explained, "and no, I don't need to go home. Here's my get out of jail free card." He dropped a 'release for work' doctor's note on my desk.

"Yeah," I nodded and pushed it back in his direction. "That would be something to see, huh? I can't wait to see you hop on your handi-capable scooter and chase the bad guys down."

He took the note back and smiled. "From what I hear, couldn't be any worse than you in a roller." He started on his casual stroll over to his desk.

"Oh ha-ha, you can go ahead and limp over to your desk and get caught up. Morning meeting is at eight o'clock.

✶✶✶✶✶✶✶✶✶

When I walked into the conference room, I just knew it was going to be standing room only. Five of the top dogs—two from the Bureau and two from ARRU—where already seated at the table. I had no idea who the fifth person was, but the old lady looked like she could hold her own in a fight.

"Sorry, are you folks having a pre-brief?" I asked. "I can wait outside the door until—"

"That won't be necessary, Agent Harris," the ARRU Director said, while looking at his counterparts as if he needed their approval somehow. "Please, have a seat."

Always gives me the creeps when one of these guys says 'please' to me. "Thanks," I said. "I guess we have quite a bit to cover?"

One of the Bureau Chiefs started punching away at the console, and then I noticed the red light above the door come on, which indicated that there was a note on the door that basically said, 'Closed Session, so stay out.'

I wondered if they were about to tear into me for something. To my surprise, there was a knock at the door. Whoever the bold person was didn't bother to wait for an answer. The door just swung open and he walked right in. It was that 'Falcon-One' character.

"Agent Harris, you know Special Agent Nance." The Chief waved him in.

Nance gave a single nod. "Oh, Agent Harris and I go way back," he said.

For a moment, I wondered how I could've trained alongside this guy for the past three months and not know his name. But, then again, they were doing their thing and we were doing ours. Humph, that's teamwork for you, but that's how it was.

His name stuck with me though; the first time that I had heard the name Nance was the same time I got the news that my friend James had met the bullet with his name on it.

"Yeah, way back," I said. "Good times, huh?"

The smile on his face slowly drifted away.

Two more people came in. It was Jay and the person I guessed to be the FBI's counterpart of the East Texas takedown.

"Come on in and take your seats gentlemen." The Bureau Director's voice had picked up a little enthusiasm. "First of all, I would like to commend you on a job well done. All objectives were met, and for all practical purposes, the organization has been dismantled; and although the remaining fractions are still on the run, it's just a matter of time before they are in custody. We've limited this meeting to the supervisors because we needed to hear your assessments of the operations before a full blown debriefing."

I started to give my interpretation, but the Lead on the East Texas Op jumped in.

"I felt it was a very smooth operation, sir. Of course, it's true that we were expecting a considerable amount more resistance; however, the lack of resistance is not something I can really complain about. It is something to be noted, though. I would say the lack of resistance could be considered an enabler toward the meeting of the objectives."

"Well," Jay said, "from an ARRU perspective, I'm gonna have to say it was a wash."

Everyone in the room had somewhat of a surprised look on their faces—except me, of course. I was used to his bluntness. "Everybody seems to think that one little mini-mobile home smoldering out there in Granger was the single point of the operation; my thinking is there are probably ten to twenty of those vehicles out there, and since we didn't find any on the grounds of the East Texas operation, well now that means we were nothing more than an inconvenience."

The Bureau Chief rubbed his right eye. I figured it was some type of stress reliever. "Agent Barnes," he said, "keep in mind, our primary mission was to take control of the facilities and dismantle the organizational structure of the Firearm Freedom Brigade. We have done this. The capture of locally manufactured relic replicas and any evidence was the secondary mission. With the 100% completion of the primary mission it's far from being a wash."

"Well, like I said, from an ARRU perspective," Jay added.

The ATF Director decided to clarify. "Everyone, bear in mind, you don't think of this operation in terms of this department or that department. The joint operation was conducted by one unit with one mission."

"I guess that means it's still a wash." I got the same looks that Jay had gotten earlier. I pointed at Jay with my thumb "Look, if what he says is true, and there are multiple mobile facilities out there, we haven't really dismantled the organization have we? I understand the wanting to give ourselves the pat on the back and pass the good word up the chain, but the fact of the matter is, the one vehicle we have identified couldn't have possibly produced the number of relic replicas we have observed on the streets, so therefore the facility is still fully functional.

True, we have the leaders of the ground facilities, but no foot soldiers, so the organizational structure is still intact. You just have new leaders."

Nance cleared his throat and joined in the conversation. "Sounds like you have a proposal, Harris. What is your recommendation?"

I put my knuckle to my upper lip as if it could help me think. "You know, with the amount of damage and the amount of potential damage that could be created by the modified mobile, I figured you guys would be in a tizzy. In any case, we definitely need to focus on the certainty of an unknown number of roaming pyro super bombs out there.

"It's obvious they do not want these vehicles captured. If given the chance, they will burn a hole into the ground. The stuff they were packing didn't need oxygen to burn, so the hunk of molten metal out there in Granger could be burning for months, if not years.

"I recommend a nationwide search. The tires should be a give-away, because due to the weight of these vehicles, standard tires will not support them. The one we chased down had military-grade tires, and they weren't put on to go joy riding on the dunes."

The Bureau Chief gave an almost silent chest laugh. "Have you considered the strain on the budget and the logistics involved in your recommendation?"

"Sure," I said. "The budget and the logistics support will be augmented by the fact that this should and will be classified as a matter of national security, so someone is going to need to do some elbow rubbing with the President and make it happen."

A new quiet in the room made me a little nervous. I started to wonder if any of the bigwigs had enough balls to say that they need some help, or were they to afraid to be seen as people who couldn't get the job done with the limited amount of resources they had.

Finally, the older, unknown lady on the right side of the Bureau Chief gave her input. "You're absolutely right, Agent Harris. It will take some time to—as you say—make it happen. Give it a couple of days for the appropriate appropriations, and we can put that new action plan in effect. That will be all, gentlemen."

I don't know who she was—she hadn't said a word since I had walked through the door, and she didn't need to look around at the other three for some mute approval. Jay and the other Team Leader stood up and got ready to make their exit.

"Well Ma'am, I don't know if we have—"

"Thank you, Agent Harris, you have direction." I suppose the ATF Director wanted to make sure I didn't put my foot in my mouth.

I shrugged and nodded like that made some kind of sense. I have direction; yeah, right.

Jay held the door open for me and followed me out. As soon as the door closed behind him, he just couldn't resist giving me some parting words to help escort me out.

"Man, you need to get your direction on outta here."

CHAPTER 9 – THE SCALES ARE BALANCED

They will curse your name and envy will course through their veins. Although you are aware of your greatness, be humble. Inspire others with the tools of success and show them the way. Chapter 6, Book of Serendipitan Values (2077)

For some reason, the bosses felt the extended search could wait; but when I looked into the eyes of Lady Gunner, I knew that whoever was left in the organization wouldn't. I sat there at my desk planning my next—

"Kyle, did you forget something?" Mercedes voice echoed irritation at the thought of my forgetting the 'we need to talk,' but she knew I hadn't. She knew I was stalling. I couldn't have had possibly forgotten something as important as us needing to talk. "I already have interrogation room B reserved for the entire day. Shall we?" I bet she really thought she was being cordial with the raised hand, palm up, in the direction of room B.

I thought about it for a second. The room was private, but motion detectors in the room would sometimes cause the audio/video equipment to kick on all by itself. Yeah, the auto-conference monitoring equipment was a little glitchy in B. "No, we shall not. Let's use conference room C."

She shrugged and then led the way.

She walked in ahead of me, and as soon as I closed the door, she turned, and I grabbed her by the waist. I pressed my lips against hers. Through the tiny slits in my eyes, I saw hands slowly rise up in the air. She didn't know whether to embrace me or to push me away.

"Stop… stop," she said finally. She gave me a gentle push, took a step back, and with a hand still on my chest, she said to me, with a shimmer in her eyes, "I want to know why you're cheating on me." It sounded more like a comment than a question. "Well, I already know why you're cheating on me, but I want to hear you say it."

"Oh, you're kidding, right? Look, there is nothin' going on between Leslie and me."

She took a step back and held up her index finger. "What?" It was a look of pure confusion. "Aw, hell, I know nothing is going on there. Besides, we had a girl-to-girl when she first got here and Leslie already knows that I would kick her ass up and down the hallways. I'm talking about you and that

Elizabeth… Whoa, see, you almost made me say the 'B' word. You just couldn't let go, huh?"

I thought I had been careful. I thought the whole situation was under control; it was a risk that seemed to be worth it at the time. I knew from the get-go that it would be hard to fool Mercedes's investigative eye, but just like so many of the criminals we bust, the crime always seems like a good idea at the time. When you're plotting the crime in your head, it sure seems like it'll be so easy to pull it off.

I knew I wouldn't be able to lie my way through this one. I knew she would see right through—

"Since you haven't answered my question yet, I'll take it as a 'No,' you couldn't let go," she said.

It was time to 'fess up. "It first started out as a 'we should remain friends' thing, and then somehow it went to 'let's talk about the problems we had,' you know… to try and get some type of closure."

"Oh, I see," she said. "And one thing led to another. So basically you're telling me you fell for the okey-doke. So which is it?" She was very calm in her demeanor.

"So which is what?" I said.

"Are you a dumb-ass, or do you take me for one?"

Since the tone in her voice became a slightly more elevated, I grabbed her hands, pressed them against my chest, and pulled her close to me. Not so much because I wanted to get all touchy-feely. As long as I was holding her hands, those hands weren't reaching for a snag or balling up into fists.

"Merce, you are not a dumb-ass. I—"

The stinging pain from the head-butt to the bridge of my nose made me stumble back about three or four steps. Hard to say when you're busy counting stars. Lucky for me, the conference room table was there, or I might have landed on my dignity.

The quiver of her top lip told me everything I needed to know about her emotional state. "I can't believe that for the past year, I've given my heart, I've given you my love, and I've basically given you full ownership of my soul. I have never done that before. I just can't believe I've given all this to a dumb-ass. Right? One of us is one, and since I'm not the dumb-ass…"

She slowly started to walk over to me. Her left hand found her back pocket. I was putting a lot of faith in the fact that Mercedes loved me, and if she pulled a snag, when she pressed it against my eyeball, she wouldn't pull the trigger.

Her hand reappeared with a handkerchief and she dabbed at the little trickle of blood just to the left of my right eye.

"Do you know how much I love you?" Her voice had gone back to being calm and soft.

"Yeah, I think I do."

"No, I think you don't." She paused, looked at the cut, and then put gentle but constant pressure on it to stop the bleeding. "You see, I know you've been seeing her for the past six weeks, but I let it go; I haven't said a word. I thought it was something that you needed to get out of your system. I just knew that we were right for each other and that we were meant to be together. I just knew you would come to your senses and realize that what you were doing was not worth risking the special thing we had. But, all of that was just the amount of love I have for you that kept the lie going inside my head. You were never going to stop. I would do anything to keep you, even let you have your fun with that— Elizabeth person." The name must've had some real power, because she pressed a little harder on the cut. "The past two weeks have been really hard on me. I wake up every morning thinking about what you've been doing with that woman, and I just feel sick to my stomach; I just get so sick.

"I can't take it anymore. Okay? Playtime is over, so you have got a decision to make about what you're going to do." She stepped back and offered me the handkerchief. Since she was so kind to offer, I took it. She wrapped her arms around my neck, and then gave me a kiss on the cheek before she turned and headed for the door.

She stood there in the doorway for a moment with her back to me. Finally, she turned and looked at me with those pretty brown eyes. "I know you'll make the right decision… Papi."

I knew she didn't mean it as a threat, but it sure sounded like one, and I felt like dirt. I felt so low that I would have to dig my way up to 'dirty low-down,' and that's pretty low. I hurt her pretty bad, and I never— why did she call me Papi? Yeah, I've heard her say it in the throes of passion, but she has never said it to me standing straight up. Was she trying to tell me something? Sick every morning for the past two weeks, and now I'm Papi? Aw, shoot.

When I grabbed the door handle, I had planned to make a straight shot over to Mercedes's desk. I exited the conference room to see the ATF Director having a conversation with Mercedes, followed by a slam of her fist on the top of her desk. It was enough to get everyone in the office to pause. She stormed off.

Unfortunately, I was between her and the exit.

When she walked past me, she shot a hard index finger. "YOUR friend. That's right, your friend," she said, and then continued toward the exit.

Glad I didn't stop and get a lottery ticket. That would have been a wasted credit, 'cause I was on a big ole' losing streak today.

I made my way over to the Director to see if I could get a little more information. The lines in his face gave me the impression he was feeling a bit more stress than usual.

"We just got word that Agrarian Mann is being released," he said. "His lawyer is processing him out as we speak. Agent Molina is going to have a final chat with him to see if she can pry any additional information out of him."

"Crap, let me guess: his lawyer is from the firm Townsend, Wilson, and Gray?"

He glanced at a document. "As a matter of fact, yes; a Tiffany Johnson from that office."

"Oh, yeah, I know Tiff," I nodded like we were old friends, but I knew Tiffany probably never wanted to ever see my face again. "Maybe I should go with her, so I—"

"Let it go, Harris. Mann will only talk to Agent Molina. If you show your face, he'll shut it down and that will be it." He turned and headed off back to his makeshift office in the main conference room.

I was left with a bag of mixed emotions. I was starting to get confused about how to feel. When Jay's fat fingers in the shape of a claw landed on my shoulder, the surprise kind of woke me up and brought me back.

Jay gave me that crooked smile. "Looks like somebody is after your girl."

Paul hobbled over, with Leslie close behind. "I've listen to the dialogue from their encounter, and I suspect he would be willing to talk to anyone from our team, but it's not worth the risk. I am certain he would talk to Merce though," Paul said. "Definitely not anyone from the Bureau; he seems to have some type of beef with those guys."

Leslie gave a shallow nod. "Maybe he just likes the ladies. Should I see if I can catch up with her? You did tell me I should co-interrogate whenever possible."

"Actually, I think he just has a thing for Mercedes," Jay said.

Paul agreed. "Yeah, for some reason he thinks they're some type of kindred spirits or something. It's like he feels he has some type of connection with her."

Jay shook his head. "Old mister Mann must be into the 'whip me, beat me' stuff. I guess he doesn't know that's your job."

I had to smile. It wasn't a sadomasochistic relationship, but Merce had her good days and her bad ones. "Alright, don't let that jealousy eat you up." I said. "Anyway, whatever fetishes I have at home need to stay out of the office." I changed the subject. "Okay, this Agrarian guy still keeps some unsavory characters for company, so we—even though she won't want it—are still going need to watch her back. Jay, Les, do you think you two can keep them at an eyeball's length? I must confess, and I have to be totally honest, if someone was to hit her in the head and drag her off, I would be very upset."

I saw Jay's mouth open, but Leslie beat him to the punch. "We're on it."

It was hard to read the expression on Jay's face. "Hey, slow down there you little 'dirt demon.' You're with me, and I'm driving," he said.

"What the… how did you get a vehicle and I can't?" I demanded.

He looked at me, one of his eyes widened, and the eyebrow slowly rose a little higher. With a straight face and a shoulder shrug, he said, "'Cause I'm better lookin'," before he walked away.

Leslie just smile, shrugged, and turned.

"You're supposed to say 'that's not true' or something like that," I insisted.

She paused and looked back at me.

"You know I'm the boss, so you're like the worst butt-kisser ever," I added.

She laughed. "I didn't have to say it; you already know it's not true."

"Thanks."

The way she laughed, I had to wonder if she detected the sarcasm in my 'thanks,' but as an interrogator, I knew it wouldn't slip past her. She just liked to flash that smile.

"So what do you think, Paul?"

He crossed his arms and made a little nod while he watched Jay and Leslie make their exit.

"Well, she has a very nice scooter."

It was at that point that I realized that since the arrival of our newest team member, both Paul and Jay had been slightly off of their game. I wondered if I was in the same situation but didn't know it.

I stepped between Paul's eyeballs and the exit. "I was referring to the takedown of the facilities, only the capture of the facility leaders, the mobile factories, the release of Agrarian Mann, so on and so forth. Is everything okay? Ordinarily, if I asked you what you thought, you would probably already have a presentation ready. Is Baker becoming a distraction?"

"What?" He looked shocked. "No, oh heck no. She's just a kid, and I was just admiring the potential. Yeah, I like her, but not in that way."

"Good, I think we both need to keep our eyes off her potential. It could cause problems for us out in the field. Besides, one office romance is enough." I was already sure that the tension between Mercedes and me would soon be spilling over into the office. "Gotta have somebody on point, and since you have the best set of eyes at seeing stuff most people miss, we're all depending on you."

A smirk wiped across his face. "You don't need to butter me up; I'm immune, and you don't get any award points for giving me a warm and fuzzy." He rolled right into an assessment. "So far we don't have much. Anderson and Johnson have been under the thumb of the Bureau, but they haven't gotten anything useful out of them. They say they want to talk, but they will only talk to the media, which could workout, since the media is trying to knock down our door to talk to them.

"I think that was the plan all along. They knew running wasn't an option. Their best option was to come here, play the martyr, and spread their message.

"You manager types and your buddies in the Bureau have a decision to make. Don't let them talk to the media and get nothing, or you can let them talk, but with that comes the risk of allowing them to become heroes to their cause and expand their following. There's even a chance of them starting a whole new movement.

"With regard to the mobile manufacturing facilities, you and I know that there is still an army of those things out there." He closed his eyes and pulled back on it. "Okay, okay, maybe not an army, but I would guess at least ten; with the amount of relics on the streets, it would have to be at least ten."

"Uh huh," I said. "With regards to the mobiles, sounds like you and Jay have been plotting on that number ten. What else?" I asked.

"Oh, Agrarian Mann. How he is walking out of here after drawing a weapon on a federal agent I have no idea," he said. "You could probably get the answer with one phone call. With regard to his agenda, it's a mystery. If it's true what he is saying about this Salvo person, sounds like there is a civil war brewing in the organization. That could be something we could use to our advantage."

I nodded and said, "Now that's the Paul we all know and love. Well, like, anyway. You're right, I'll make the call."

****

Marcus was a busy man, so I didn't expect to get through on the first try. I was more surprised that he hadn't called me to let me know that his firm was representing Agrarian Mann. After all, he along with his wife and daughter were just in my house a week ago. The six of us had a nice Sunday dinner. I guess you could say that Mercedes and his wife had things in common, resting on opposite ends of the fun list, but his daughter AlaSundra and Hannah had become like sisters.

I know that he has an obligation to his clients, but he could have at least thrown me a bone. I shouldn't be surprised, though. The guy had to be represented by someone, and I knew that he had the funds.

I suppose I was ready for a fight, because the chime of the phone didn't take me by surprise, and I didn't waste any time tearing into Marcus. "Marcus, what is the—"

The soft voice on the other end sounded more like gloating. "Sorry, Agent Harris. This is Tiffany Johnson. It's my understanding that you had some questions regarding my client, Agrarian Mann. How can I help you?"

"Oh, hi, Tiff. What? No pleasantries? Not even a how are you, or how's the kids?"

Tiffany didn't like me one bit. She didn't like the relationship I had with her boss, and I was just working class. She saw herself as a future partner, and I was just some nobody that needed to provide law enforcement services for her.

"I think it best if we keep this professional," she said. "I'm only returning the call as a courtesy for Mister Townsend. I should really only be discussing this, or any issue related to my client, with the District Attorney."

"I understand, Tiff. I won't take too much of—"

"Sir, my name is Tiffany Johnson; I would appreciate it if you addressed me as such."

I wanted to laugh, but recent events had put me in kind of a somber mood. "Yeah, I could talk to the D.A., too, but I was hoping to get the perspective of the other team."

I thought I was being very tactful; however, Tiffany remained fixed on being my adversary.

"Well," she said. "I'll share with you this. Everything Townsend, Wilson, and Gray does and will do is in the best interest of our client. Agrarian Mann is a leader of the community, and if you had talked to the D.A., you would have known that the interaction with Agent Molina was a complete misunderstanding. By law, he was required to disclose that he was transporting a collector's item. The snafu on the part of our client is admitted by not presenting the transportation documentation first.

"Come on, Agent Harris; do you think the D.A. is really going to put a fine upstanding citizen in confinement because Agent Molina refused to allot him the time to show the required paperwork, which he had on his person?

"Our client came in on his own accord to assist you with your investigation, and this is how he is treated. I'll have you know civil action is seriously being considered at this point in time."

Yeah, I couldn't see it, but I could just sense that giant crocodile smile on the other end of the line. I started to switch over to sarcasm, but I decided to let her have her day. "Thanks, Tiffany Johnson, you have been more than helpful."

She knew it was her day, so I understood the need to rub it in. "Oh and just so you know, this is my way of showing very little respect to your home. This is how I come into your house and make myself at home."

I know the cut was a reference to that day when I walked through her office like I owned it to get what I needed. Since she wanted to play tough, I couldn't hold back any more. "Just so you know," I said, "we're even and the scales are balanced. So now our futures dictate our paths." Thought I'd leave her with something she would understand; a simple quote straight out of the Book of Serendipitan Values. I guess the quote gave her pause.

"Well… is there anything else I can help you with, Agent Harris?" she asked.

"Oh no, I think you have been more than helpful. Thank you." It's never a good phone call when you feel like you enjoyed the sound of the disconnect.

In any case, I hadn't gained any real ground, and Agrarian was back on the street to continue with whatever plan he had in motion.

I liked the idea of a civil war though. It would make it a lot easier to clean up after the smoke and ashes.

CHAPTER 10 – SPLATTER PATTERNS

There was a time when the longbow was considered a miraculous technological achievement for its day. Its day has come and gone. What hasn't gone is the desire to control our own destinies and the power to command our own fates. You will never take my relics. You might as well cut out my soul. Lenard Anderson, President, Texas Liberty League of Arms (2092)

I guess there are worse things than being chained to a hospital bed. I can honestly say it was one of the better nights I spent in custody.

I don't think I could've received a nicer surprise than Agent Molina at the nurse's station on my way out.

"Oh my," I said. "Did you come to see me? You do know visiting hours ended about ten minutes ago. If you're not careful, Agent Molina, you're going to make me start to feel special." I finally got half a smile out of her.

"Yeah well, I figured since I sent you here, I should see you out."

It was almost bewitching, the spell she had over me. It scared me the things I knew and the things she wanted to know. I imagined a relationship between the two of us could be hazardous to the cause. The problem was, I believed it would be hard to deny her anything.

"Please… walk with me?" I asked.

"Sure," she said, with a step to the side, leading her hand in the direction of the exit.

We started to walk, passing the two individuals in the lobby from the FFB sent to pick me up. They tried to blend in, but it was obvious to me who they were even though they had not said a word in an effort not to give their purpose away. I wondered if Molina recognized them.

"I take it this visit isn't because you were concerned over my well-being."

The half-smile was gone. "I suppose there are still a few items we need to clear up." She leaned over and whispered, "Maybe we need to wait until we get out of earshot of your lackeys back there."

I couldn't resist a half-smile of my own. "Well, nothing I've told you is of a covert nature. I've really only let you know that I hope to put an end to this stranglehold on freedom called the Gun Control Act through political and legal action. I believe this can be done because our cause is just; however, there are some who wish to pursue a much more nefarious agenda."

She shot me a look somewhere between caution and curiosity. "You know, I'm starting to wonder if I could be wrong about you." She waved it off, "Oh, that whole idea is just plain silly. I'm a woman; I'm never wrong."

We both laughed for a moment, and it seemed all the tension between us melted away.

"I think, perhaps another time and place… well, we could have been really good friends," I said, and I felt a pathetic, boyish look creep across my face. She was a tough girl, and I hoped whatever she saw in my face didn't come across to her as some kind of weakness.

She drifted back into her half smile. "Listen," she said, "we may not be good friends, but we don't have to be enemies. We both have chosen our paths in this life. We could start by giving a little respect to the choices."

The quick eye shift in the direction of the two men that had come to pick me up was barely noticeable.

"I can't think of a better place to start," I said.

She placed her hand on my shoulder and turned me in the direction of the exit. We left through the main doors into the lobby, and the small talk she made couldn't hide the way her eyes constantly scanned the surroundings. I don't think she missed a thing.

"Are we in any immediate danger?" she asked.

"What? Those guys? Oh no, they're just my ride. They may look like a couple of shady characters up to no good, but that's just the look that comes with the charge of my personal safety."

"I see. Well, okay, here's what I think. I think the hospital halls and walls are a perfect echo chamber, and no matter how careful or how low we whisper, someone is going to have ears on. Maybe we should just have a seat in my vehicle and finish up, clear up anything that may have gotten missed."

"Agent Molina, I—"

"Call me Mercedes."

"Well, Mercedes, to be honest, I do and have enjoyed these short periods of time we have spent together. Although the offer sounds tempting, you see, I already have this big bruise on the side of my face, and I represent some kind of role model to some, so I can't afford to go home with a black eye as well. You see, I've developed sort of a crush on you, and sitting in a car with you like a couple of teenagers… well, I would be tempted to put my hand on your thigh."

She laughed out loud. I think it was the first time I had seen her close her eyes that wasn't a blink. "Oh you wouldn't have to worry about that. Sitting in the car is kind of awkward, and I don't think I could get the leverage for a black-eye shot; in any case, I do keep one hand on the BISCIT."

"Oh, your brain inhibitor thing; I don't know if that's better or worse. I suppose it could be better: while I'm in a coma, you could take advantage of me."

She laughed again. "Sorry, I'm the kind of girl that likes interaction and mutual satisfaction. You would need to be awake for me to get any pleasure out of the situation. Oh and sober, awake and sober is my deal."

I grabbed her hand and squeezed it softly. "Thanks for that little tidbit of information. You know, everyone deserves a few pleasures in life. Now I feel I have some tools to help you achieve some; unfortunately, with that information I think I will be tossing and turning at night for the next week or so."

"Only a week or so, eh?" In somewhat of a playful manner, she grabbed her forehead and then shook her head. "Sounds like I'm losing my touch."

I couldn't help myself. With my index finger, I took a chance and touched the backside of her hand. I slowly moved the length of the hand down to the wrist. I admired the lines and the beauty of them.

There was a moment of hesitation before she pulled away. She stepped back and attempted to regain her composure.

"Agrarian, I'm supposed to be messing with your head; you're not supposed to be messing with mine," she said. "We've already talked about that."

"Uh huh, well…" I walked over to the information desk and got a pamphlet and pen. I looked back at her, and she had gone back to that hard-as-steel expression she had had when I first walked into her office. I walked back over and handed her the pamphlet. "Here is my personal number. Call me— professionally or personally, it doesn't matter. Just call me. In three days, I will be heading back to New York. I can't think of anything I would like more than… well, I would be more than happy to make myself available for private interrogations."

I turned and walked away; I didn't need to look back. I already knew she was having mixed feelings. I wished I could have given her more. If I gave her any more, I would be walking a fine line on my oath and obligation to my people and my cause. I was limited by law… laws I personally created as to what I could disclose.

I felt the piercing of her eyes burning the exposed skin on the back of my neck, and it felt good. Could I turn her to our cause? Probably not, but I was certain that this was the beginning of a relationship that would blossom into more than just a squeeze of the shoulder and the pat of a hand.

I'm not done with you, Mercedes Molina.

****

The extra safety measures added to the trip made the ride to our destination a lot longer than it should have been. First, a couple of hours in the city, riding in circles to make sure we weren't being followed and then two underground garage detours for transport changes to eliminate the possibility of a tracking device.

I spent the majority of the time observing the skill set and training of my two escorts. They were exceptionally well trained and disciplined. Ordinarily, I would admire such a thing; however, lately, the training I've seen being delivered at some of our facilities was nowhere close to the level of training that these two had shown.

"You two are not just the run of the mill. Are you FFB Spec Ops?"

Even from the back seat, I saw no change in their expressions. They were focused and on mission. It was not unexpected that they would send the best they had to come get me; especially since I had dispatched my personal guards to assist with the recovery efforts after the feeble attempt to dismantle our organization.

I felt caution, even though they had each given me a snag for my personal protection. The first thing I did during that initial two hours was disassemble and check the weapons. They were fully functional—for whatever that's worth in snag world—and giving a fully functional weapon is not the first thing you do with a guy like me if you want to take my life.

The escort on the passenger side turned to answer my question. "No, Sir, we were contracted to ensure that you make it to your destination safely. We are not members of the Firearm Freedom Brigade."

"I see. If not from the FFB, I'm still curious where you guys received your training."

"Well, I received most of my training in the service. I served for eight years and participated in various campaigns throughout the world. As world order began to fall into place, I could always count on discord and dissention in the good ole' U.S. of A. to provide opportunities. I guess you could say we're freelancers now."

"Say no more." That was plenty. "I know who you guys are. Wow, the council must really want me to make this meeting if they spent hard earned credits to cover your fees."

The guy on the passenger side returned forward and continued to scan the streets and buildings.

"I reckon, Sir."

I reckon, Sir. Said like a true minster of death. Everyone on the council knew that I didn't tolerate their kind of dirty business, but one thing was for certain, I would make my destination. Still, I drew the two snags that were given me and allowed them to rest between my knees, pointing at the floorboard.

I leaned back and drifted off. I was sure that both of these guys were just as fast—if not faster—than Mercedes, and if they wanted me dead, I would have been so a long time ago.

Still… I took some comfort, and in fact, held it as sort of a security blanket that the little amber lights had flipped over to green.

****

Finally, after all the diversionary tactics and caution, we arrived at our destination. They drove down into the parking area of an underground garage. I knew the place; in fact, I had been here before. It had been a long time ago, but I knew exactly where we were going.

They started their spiral downward, two levels, and in between the second and third they came to a quick stop in front of a maintenance door. At first glance, you would have thought it was just an access to an air conditioner maintenance unit, but it was much more than that.

The guy in the passenger seat turned again. "It has been a pleasure doing business with you, Sir; but this is where our contract ends."

"I see." I figured the snags where just loaners, so I put them together and held them out for him, butt first.

"Keep them," he said. "The price of the weapons was included in our contract. Oh, and the people that requested our services are not aware of that fact, so…" he put his index finger up to his lips. "Shhh…."

I gave him a single nod and mimicked his finger to the lips.

I concealed the weapons in readymade holsters that were sewn into pretty much my entire wardrobe. As soon as I closed the car door, they sped down the spiral driveway, disappearing deeper into the garage.

The maintenance door opened, and there in the doorway stood the team leader whose arm I had snapped several days ago, offering me safe passage. His arm was still in a brace, and I have to believe there was still some pain there. He looked at me and then massaged the elbow.

Our eyes only connected for a moment before he looked away. He feigned the scanning of his surroundings, but I knew the cameras and motion detectors had this area secured to within 300 feet.

"Hey Agrarian, they're waiting for you in the conference room."

As soon as the door closed behind us, I turned and grabbed his good shoulder. "Listen, I know you could probably kick me in the prunes, but I just wanted you to know that I am sorry for… this thing here. I hope you understand; the last month or so has been very difficult, but—"

"No need to apologize, Commander. I know that you are the kind of guy to get the job done, no matter what it takes." He seemed to genuinely understand, but still refused to look me directly in the eye. Normally, I would have reprimanded such behavior, but I thought I had already alienated this guy enough. I decided to let it pass.

Excellent. I saw they had managed to salvage a fair amount of equipment—equipment that would keep the dream alive. Many of the faces I saw were familiar from my travels to remote facilities throughout the country.

I was filled with a sense of pride when they clapped as I made my way through the room. First two people, and then several; finally, everyone was giving a round of applause. Damned impressive. Yes, they had something to be proud about. They had left the Bureau scratching their heads and still in a tizzy.

I was sure the council was riding on a cloud right now. Everything we'd worked for, all the pieces, were falling into place. Damned impressive, I had to say.

I couldn't get enough of the excitement. The elation from the success of our evolution that everyone exhibited was contagious. It felt like I was walking on air.

It was a long walk through the main area to the other side where the offices were, but the excitement in the air made the trip seem like nothing. I gave everyone one last victory wave as I entered the office area hallway.

"What's your name, son?" Although several of his teeth were showing signs of early rot, as well as his breath, his smile seem genuine enough.

"Randal, Sir, but my secret name is Grip."

"Randal, that's what I'm fighting for. Soon enough, we'll be seeing real gun owners dancing in the streets with the same excitement." I grabbed the door handle to the conference room and turned it while I continued my rant. "You are about to bear witness to the voice of change. This thing that we've set in motion has taken on a life of its own. Once we—"

I had to stop and catch my breath.

Inside the conference room was nothing but the work of pure evil. I felt the blood drain from my face, but the shock only lasted for a moment; the shock became anger.

There were four other members on our council. There were four bodies scattered throughout various locations in the conference room. It was obvious they had been tortured extensively before what was apparently a grisly demise. Two of them were still bound to office chairs with their throats slit.

The practice had come to be known as a FFB super happy because of the smile it represented. They had started to appear about a year ago, about the same time Salvo started spewing his opposition to our methods and we first received rumors of a splinter group.

My other two colleagues lay at opposite ends of the room, face down, and without even seeing the gaping wounds, from the amount of blood I knew they had also been extended the same courtesy.

And Salvo, in his wallow of egocentric insanity, sat comfortably in a chair, which he had placed on top of the conference room table.

"Come on in, Commander. I've… or should I say we've… been waiting on you."

I heard the door close behind me. I didn't want to take my eyes off Alonso, so I turned my head to the side and looked over my shoulder. I saw my brand new friend Randal pull a relic from his brace.

"Yeah, so you're sorry, huh? I bet you're real sorry now," he said.

"Randal!" Alonso's chair scooted forward an inch or so from the shout. "This is still The Commander, and you will give respect where respect is due."

The power that Randal held in his right hand deserved a certain level of respect also; however, I held very little regard for the character of what was obviously a very tiny man. I returned my attention to Alonso. Salvo was the real threat in the room.

I drove deeper into the room as I continued my conversation with the man, stepping over the body of my fellow council member while I slowly

made my way around the table to get a better
position.

"Have you gone insane, Alonso?" I asked. "Is
this part of your grand plan? Kill all the council
members, and everyone in the organization is
supposed to cheer for you and embrace you as their
savior?"

"Now, didn't I just give a speech about giving
respect where it was due? I'm the one in charge," he
said, and then pulled out a 9MM relic, pearl handle.

Boy, is he going to be mad as hell when I take it from
him.

"Besides," he continued. "I'm not the one who
killed them. You did. Maybe not by your own hand,
but you gave the order to the captain of your
personal guard." The smile and expression on his
face gloated on how proud he was in his cleverness.
"At least, that's what I'm going to tell everyone," he
said. "They have already made their escape; but, we
are in the process of hunting them down."

It shouldn't have, but this thing with Salvo
caught me by surprise. I couldn't allow this plan of
his to move any further, not another inch.

I envisioned the whole scenario. It had to be
fast. It would be just a blur.

"Let me, Salvo, let me do him." The ranting of
Randal was all the distraction I needed.

"What was it you said?" Randal asked. "Oh,
you were going to give me a break, and then you—"

By the time my right shoulder touched the
ground, I already had my hands on the pistol grips of
the two weapons I was given. When I came out of

the roll, I was already underneath the table. The round fired by Alonso sent fragments of oak flying in every direction. Missed.

My weapon was already center mass on Randal before I finished the roll. The two rounds hit him in the chest before I pinned my elbows against the floor and put a volley of rounds into the bottom of the table.

I couldn't see him, but I could tell he was moving quickly to the right. I moved left.

It sounded like he was rolling toward the edge of the table; I was sure he was going to roll off, so I leaped and slid on top. I don't know if the single round I put under the table connected or not, but I had no time. I saw an opening.

One leap put me halfway to the door. When I landed, I grabbed a chair and slung it hard in the direction Alonso most likely lay to make sure he didn't have a clear shot while I made a break for it. When I turned back toward the door, the wild round that that damned Randal—still clinging to life— managed to get off tore through the fleshy part of my right shoulder. The shock instinctively caused me to continue the spin, so I went with it.

I allowed myself to spin 360, and when I came out of the spin, the blur of Randal's face sat like a silhouette at the other end of my front and rear sights. When his head exploded, I knew that the contractors had known what I would be walking into. They had set me up with hollow points.

I had been slowed a bit, but I could still make it. I knew Alonso was probably honing in on me, so I dropped the weapon from my right hand and made a grab for the door handle. I allowed my left arm to swing down and back. Holding the weapon upside-down, I started to shoot blindly while I attempted to make my escape.

The spatter pattern on the door let me know that I hadn't made it. I didn't feel it; it just suddenly became hard to breathe.

The next round created the momentum that caused me to push the door back closed. I couldn't get my legs to work anymore. I didn't feel my kneecaps hit the floor, but I knew I was on them. It seemed like the whole world got bigger after I made the sudden stop from the drop.

I still had some fight in me, though. My head and shoulders turned in Alonso's direction. My brain said that I had already lifted the weapon and fired, but my eyes saw my arm still dangling at my side. It hadn't moved an inch. I had almost made it out, but that damned Randal spoiled the plan.

Even though I still felt I had some fight left, apparently Alonso saw something different. He casually walked in my direction. He obviously saw me as no threat, since he felt comfortable enough to pull the magazine from his weapon, count rounds, and reload while he took a leisurely stroll-in-the-park walk in my direction.

"I hope you realize your plan is doomed to fail," I said.

His eyes widened, and then went blank for a moment while he imagined the possibilities. "Hum," he said. "I hope you realize—before you go—that even with all your high and mighty, all-for-the-cause preaching, you're the villain in this story. I'm the hero; I've come to save the day. Really now… 'Your plan is doomed to fail,' how cliché. More to the point, on the statement you just made, that's exactly what you would say to a super villain." His eyes looked like they lit up with pride on that comment. He shook his head. "Truth be told, at least my plan has got a chance. For the past twenty years, the government has refused to even sit down at the table with you people. You really think this year will be different?"

He raised his arm, and I was staring down the barrel of destiny.

All that I had worked for, my cause, my life; it was all so clear now. It was all so fragile and it was about to become just another fragment of broken glass on the pavement from a two-story window.

If nothing else, I still had the right to go with a little dignity. That's it, swallow any fear. He had won, but there would be no begging, no groveling. I needed to let him know that he hadn't beaten me.

"Salvo, you are a petty, narcissistic muther fu—
"

CHAPTER 11 – IT'S ALL UNDER CONTROL

There are enough laws on the books already, we don't need any more. When you think about it, we might be better off with a clean slate. The only laws we really need are treat each other with respect and dignity. Jerry Sandersaul, Chairman, Firearm Freedom Brigade (2075)

I was in awe, to say the least. To tell the truth, I didn't really know how to feel. I sat there at my desk, looking at the promotion and transfer approval of the new Team Leader of the Seattle Office. I had seen the position listed on the board, but I didn't even know Mercedes had applied for it.

The promotion was provisional, but effective immediately. She had been promoted from GS10 to GS12, and was authorized a three-week vacation before she had to jump into that role as boss of ARRU-12 up there.

All kinds of mixed emotions were messing with my head. Yeah, that was the biggest problem with getting so emotionally caught up on the job. The most confusing thing, she had to have put in for this position—oh yeah, about the same time as when Elizabeth and I started our thing. Oh, crud.

Maybe it was just my ego; more so, maybe it was the guilt that caused me to think this way. Maybe this was something she had been wanting all this time but kept hidden and bottled up inside.

My thoughts were that this was one of those things that she probably wouldn't share with me. But, now that that cat had clawed its way out of the bag, I'd have all the dirty details in a minute.

She came through the door and motored herself between the desks in her typical Mercedes fashion. She approached my desk, so I stood ready to get a little Q&A, but she continued past without giving me a second glance. If she had only seen me shake my head at all of that nonsense, she would have made it a point to turn around and give me a little conversation, whether I wanted it or not.

I grabbed my chair and rolled it over next to her desk.

"I have extra chairs around my desk you could have sat at," she said.

"Yeah, but I like my chair. None of those other chairs have the backside support my little sit-downs require. I'm not as young as I used to be, you know."

I just got a nod. "How can I help you, Agent Harris?"

I dropped my head and started to laugh. Whatever humor I found in the situation, she didn't feel it. "Merce, what's going on? Things have never been this tense between us. Okay, what can I do to make it right?"

"If I have to tell you," she said, "there's absolutely nothing that can be done." Her eyes fell to her desk and she continued scribbling on a pad.

"I see. Alright, well let me throw a hook out there and let's see if I get a bite."

She continued to ignore me.

"I know you're a bad ass, but still I've hurt you pretty bad."

I still got nothing.

"And, you've invested all this time, energy, and your heart and soul in this relationship, but you're beginning to wonder if you're wasting your time."

Her eyes popped up,

"As well as if I'm even serious about your needs and the future of this relationship."

She leaned back in her chair and was now looking directly at me. The look in her eyes said, 'Please be in love with me,' so I kept going. "I know, I know it all felt so magical and you thought that by now we would be married, living happily ever after. Maybe even starting our own little family. I have to be honest with you; I have no intention on asking you to marry me." Boy, the whirlwind of expressions in her face with that comment made me wanna jump back, but I held my ground until I finished. "At least until you make a decision on what you want to do about this."

I handed her the new appointment to Seattle and the air she sucked in to her mouth must have made her ears pop.

"YEAH!" she jumped up. The realization of what this actually meant to our relationship slowly put a strangle hold on her excitement.

"What?" I asked, "This is what you wanted. Right?"

"This IS what I wanted," she responded. Merce put the paper on top of the desk. "Mostly."

"I'm glad. You know I will support you in whatever you decide, so let me know what you plan on doing." I didn't bother to stand. I gave the floor a good push and rolled my chair back toward my desk.

"You didn't really ask me," she said.

I'm sure I probably looked stumped.

She started to shout across the room, but then looked at everyone staring at her. She grabbed the paper and walked over to me for a little privacy. "You were telling me how you felt, and then you gave me this half-assed ultimatum, but you never asked me to… you know. How am I supposed to make a decision with only half the information?"

I smiled, stood, and pushed the chair the rest of the way over to my desk. "Merce, you do what is right for you. Follow your dreams or follow your heart, whatever that may be. Maybe it's a little of both. Only you can say. I don't want to tell you what I think you should do. I don't want to influence your decision. I have no doubt you will make the best decision for you." I turned to continue my little journey back to my desk. Every step seemed heavier and heavier. Once I finally reached my desk, I understood that the thing that was slowing me down was my soul being torn apart.

I knew that once she left, I might have to leave too. There was no way I could do this job; I couldn't be as effective without her. I would no longer be whole.

I knew I wouldn't ever be able to get my mind right, and I would be placing the lives of whoever I worked with in jeopardy.

She came the rest of the way over to my desk, leaned over, and whispered in my ear. "All of that dancing and side-stepping around the question, but you still haven't asked me. You just make me so damned mad sometimes." She turned and went back to her desk.

✳✳✳✳✳✳✳✳✳✳

Jay and Leslie came through the door and for some reason stopped at the reception desk. That was the hot-spot, and there was always something going on in the office, but Edith hadn't stopped them. They first looked at me and then Mercedes.

Paul approached them and started up a conversation. He wasn't kind enough to face my direction while he was talking, so I wasn't able to decipher whatever it was he was telling them, and then they all turned and looked at me and then Mercedes.

I shot them all a middle finger. At that point, Jay shrugged, mouthed the words, 'Not my business,' and headed over toward his desk. Leslie gave me only half of one of those patented smiles she normally throws out there. At this point, the way things were going, I was just going to roll with the punches.

For some unknown reason, the office suddenly became a hive of activity. The armorers all started moving to the equipment room. Some were already geared up and coming out.

"Alright folks, let's move it. We got to roll." The MARRV Team Leader looked a little annoyed that everyone hadn't gotten geared up as fast as she had. I was annoyed that somehow, with whatever was going on, I had been kept out of the loop.

I checked my phone. As fate would have it, the phone was dead. Instead of fussing over the thing, I decided to just grab somebody in the know.

"Hey what's going on?" I caught one of the armorers just before he managed to get out of the door.

"Harris, I thought you would've already been out the door and on your way to the scene."

I didn't have to say anything; I'm sure the confused look on my face told him to keep going and hurry up.

"They found five people dead with an unknown number of relics," he explained. "Three men and two women, but the thing you would probably be most concerned about is one of them was that Agrarian Mann guy."

It was more of a curiosity than a shock for me.

"You ready to go?" Jay came up on my right side.

"Yeah, I just need to grab a couple of things and then—" the look on Mercedes face made me freeze in my tracks.

I looked at Jay and pointed in her direction with the side of my head. Her reaction to the news looked like it made him kinda nervous. For Jay, that's a big leap.

I walked over to her desk, with Jay close behind.

"You look a little shook up there, Merce. What's the deal?"

She stood there trying to swallow the news. Jay and I looked at each other, and then back to her.

"What? I… What are you two just standing there gawking at?" she asked. "We got a job to do so let's just get it done." She grabbed the Director's vehicle keycard off the desk. "I got a car; you riding with me or what?"

"I guess it's me, you, and Leslie," I said. "Paul, are you up to a limp over to Jay's car?

Mercedes simply walked away.

Jay leaned a little closer to my ear. "I don't know what's going on with you two, but I could have sworn she was about to burst into tears at any second."

I had noticed the same thing, but I know that it wasn't anything that was going on between her and me. "Yes, well, she has been going through a lot lately. But, don't you worry your big ass mouth about it. It's all under control."

He nodded. "Sure hope so."

I turned in Leslie's direction. "You ready, Baker?"

She threw her hands out to the sides and then let them drop to slap the sides of her thighs. "Waiting on you… Kyle."

I held up my phone. "You go ahead and catch up with Merce, but don't let that Mercedes leave without me. I have to switch out the battery, and I better not have to chase y'all down in a roller."

She laughed and since I gave her the opening, she couldn't resist. "Now see that's a scary thought."

I walked over to my desk and dropped the phone into the battery changer. I heard the gizmos inside hum, the light finally changed to green, and then the phone popped up like a piece of toast. Seem like a bit of overkill, but with the new media devices you couldn't charge or change the battery yourself. It had to be done with the drop box. Just another way for the company to put their hands in my pockets, I suppose.

****

I don't know if it was the latest events that were creating this cruddy thunk of a feeling in my gut, but the ride was really depressing. Leslie sat in the back, tapping away at her phone with an occasional look out the window. Merce drove down the road like the weight of the world was resting on her shoulders.

"Alright," I said. "This is bull-crap. What's going on, Merce?"

"What do you mean?"

I shook my head, because she knew exactly what I was talking about. "This… I'm talking about this somebody just kicked my dog mood that you're in."

"I don't know what you're talking about."

"Fine," I said. "You say everything's good, well then it must be good."

We continued down the road and about thirty seconds later, I made another attempt at casual conversation. "Well, at least we got rid of that asshole Agrarian Mann.

The car swerved in the lane; Mercedes managed to get control of the car, and at the same time punched her finger in my face.

"Hey, there was nothing wrong with Ag. He was okay. At least, when he lied to me it was to make a point. Not for some sneaky, underhanded personal need that he needed to fill." She could've made a donation with the amount of blood bulging from the vein on the right side of her neck.

"Hey, look," Leslie jumped in, with a soft, almost submissive tone. "Paul and Jay are pulling over."

Mercedes started to slow down and Leslie had the car door open before Merce even came to a complete stop. "I'll go see what they want," Leslie said.

I watched her walk over to the passenger side to have a chat with Paul. She looked back, gave a smile and a big ole' thumbs up that everything was okay, and then got in the back seat.

"Oh, that fucking cow," Mercedes had to laugh at her own comment. "They didn't want anything; it's what she wanted."

I watched as they slowly pulled back into the traffic. "Can you blame her?" I sent them a message 'not to wait up' on us. "Alright, Merce. Put it in park, and let's take a break. Maybe we need to clear the air and get some stuff off our chests."

She took her hands off the wheel and foot off the brake and the car's sensors placed the vehicle in park mode. When she folded her arms across her chest and placed her back against the car door, I got the feeling she really wanted to talk, but I would have to get this thing started.

"Alright," I began, "I don't know what this thing that you and Mister Mann had going on, but whatever it was, or whatever you think it could have been, it is nothing compared to what you and I have been through. I get it; I've hurt you and I don't know if you can ever forgive me, but whatever this relationship holds, you can't… no, *we* can't let this thing fester inside your soul."

"I can forgive you, Kyle. I can forgive you, and I can't forgive you. What I mean is if I knew where I really stood and where we were going, it could be so easy to forgive you, but I feel so lost. You and that Beth… person had a thing for a lot of years; you even had wedding plans. Now, I find out that you two have started to build something special again and here I am… I'm just dangling on a string… just blowing in the wind... I'm scared, Kyle. I'm so scared I don't know what to do. I'm having nightmares; I wake in a cold sweat and so petrified in the mornings that I become sick to my stomach."

"Oh, so you're not pregnant?" I asked. First, I got a look of confusion, and then it went off like a light bulb.

"Oh, this morning, when I told you I get sick... you thought—you will be happy to know that you're not going to be a new papa. Well, not with me anyway."

"What makes you think that would make me unhappy? You would make a great mom." I saw hope once again fill her eyes. She just needed some type of assurance that my little relapse with Elizabeth was a lapse in judgment, and I had come to my senses. She just wanted to know that it was over and now it was just me and her against the world. I would take her in my arms and when I held her she would know at that moment she was the most important person in the world.

I opened my arms and moved for the embrace, but the moment of passion was interrupted when the palm of her hand wrapped around my nose and her fingers circled and cupped the rest of my face.

"What are you doing?" she said. "Are you trying to sneak up on me?" The warmth of my own breath bounced off her hand and back onto my face. "Haven't you figured out I'm onto your tricks by now? You're trying to play with my emotions."

"I'm trying to let you know that no matter what mistakes I've made in the past and all the mistakes—and you can bet I will—that I'll make in the future, my heart and soul belongs to you."

She dropped her hand. "All you had to do was say so."

The embrace that followed was unlike any I had felt before. Even the cars that drove by blowing their horns couldn't put a damper on the mood.

We finally caught up with the remainder of the team at the scene. First things first, of course, we needed to protect the crime scene. We went through the standard rituals.

I guess they couldn't wait on us, since they were already in the process of capturing an image set. Leslie was busy on the outside, somewhere between capturing the exterior and charming the armorers that were standing guard with that smile of hers. I just assumed Paul and Jay to be getting the scoop on the inside.

They already had momentum, so I decided not to interrupt. Mercedes and I could just follow up behind. Maybe with the third and fourth sets of eyeballs, we might pick-up on something that may have gotten skipped.

"I'm guessing that you and the Ag Mann were developing some kind of friendship." I said. "Are you okay with this?"

Mercedes just didn't seem her usual self on the scene. She shot me a sneer, "Are you kidding? No, we were not developing a friendship. I told him I had a man, but that my man was just behaving badly right now."

"That's not what I meant. I meant two people on opposite sides; two people with some mutual respect for each other, that kind of stuff." There was a hint of guilt on her face, not sure why. "So he was hitting on you?"

She smile and leaned in closer and whispered, "Now you know it's not nice to kiss and tell." She started to walk toward the office building.

"Is that right? I hope your kiss and tell is not that he kissed you and you're not telling."

"Oh, really now? You have some nerve—" She almost ran over Detective Hernandez coming out of the building.

"Slow down there, Agent Molina, everything is under control," he said.

"Tell me something, Alonso," I asked. "Do you ever get sick of the smell of rotting bodies? I mean, you have to consider a career change every now and then."

"Harris, you should thank your lucky stars I'm on the case. Hell, I practically solve half your cases for you. You guys keep Homicide busier than anyone else. If it wasn't for you guys and your ridiculous gun laws, I would be out of business."

I had always felt Alonso's humor a little on the dry-side, but I had to laugh. "You know how this works: I'm just on the job making sure everyone is doing what they're supposed to. We're all chasing the bad guys. Besides, they're not my laws. I was too young to vote at the time. I just enforce them."

"I hear you," he said.

"Well, do you have anything that's going to make this one a little easier?" Mercedes asked.

Alonso looked back at the building, where I guessed the victims lie before he spoke. "You guys know I'm a generous man. I don't mind sharing, so I'll tell you what I know. The four victims inside where not done here. Can't say where at this time, but they were definitely moved here, so I'm guessing all the relics lying about had to be moved here also. I don't have a fancy ARRU title, but it's obvious the relics were staged for you. Seems like they really wanted to rub it in your faces."

"Thanks for the personal insight," I said.

"Hey, I call it as I see it."

"Three men and two women, right?" Mercedes asked.

"That's what it looks like, but who can tell these days?" He scanned Mercedes's lean muscular frame.

"Uh huh. Let me know once you get done admiring."

He gave a little laugh. "I'm all done."

"I have no doubt you've already identified the victims. I don't want to know their names; I'm more interested in any alias you may have come across. Has the name 'Salvo' passed within earshot lately?"

"What kind of name is that?" Alonso asked. "Are you sure that's a name? Sounds like some kind of fancy margarita maker."

Mercedes closed her eyes and shook her head. "I'll take that as a no."

"Should I dig a little deeper on that? I mean, if it's something that will help me crack this mystery, I'm on it. My desk is starting to get buried under relic-related bull... sorry, no offence."

Mercedes slowly turned and walked away while she spoke, "Let's just say I don't know if it's relevant to this particular incident, but I'm pretty damned sure it's related."

Alonso turned and gave me a shrug. "I guess this Salvo character is some kind of bad dude, huh?"

I gave him a stone-faced shrug back. "Yeah, well, the jury is still out on that one."

He nodded and continued past me. "Okay," he said. "Well let me know if there's anything we can do to help."

I think I liked him better when he was an asshole. Normally, he wouldn't lift a finger to help us out. I guess all the pressure from the brass coming from the top down on the joint operation did have some advantages.

"So you coming or what?" Mercedes's little almond head was the only thing that came out of the door. Sounded like she missed me.

"Right behind you."

I could tell that Jay and Paul were wrapping up. Jay was securing the imaging pack, and Paul was sending the information he had on the locations of all the relics they found to the armorers for inventory and collection.

"Y'all late, so y'all can go on back out now. We're all done." Jay always had to give his little two cents. I knew he wasn't serious, but even after all these years it seemed Mercedes still had a little trouble reading him. Well, maybe she could but she didn't care.

"Somebody has got to check up on you," she said. He laughed at her, and I saw the tenseness in her shoulders melt away. She gave a slow nod. "Where's the victims, Jay?"

I suppose the seriousness in her face was the reason his smile slowly faded away. "Third office on your right."

After she left to investigate, Jay kind of slid over next to me and whispered. "Are you two alright?"

"Yeah, we're good."

"Shoot." He stepped away and went back to being loud and slightly obnoxious. "I suppose you two are gonna go back to making all the cooing noises in the office huh? Oh baby-baby, oh baby-baby; don't nobody wanna be listening to that noise every day."

"Alright, let's not get carried away. Some folks just got to exaggerate everything."

Paul snuck up on my left. "Sorry to tell you, but it's more fact than fiction. You know my desk is right next to Merce's and some of the pet sounds that come up when you come over can make a person a little queasy."

"Oh, I see you two are trying to gang up on me. Y'all are just mad because Leslie treats the both of you like leprosy leftovers."

They looked at each other, and then back at me. I realized they were serious. I thought I had that part of the relationship under complete control, but apparently not.

"Okay, alright," I said. "Tell you what: yeah we are okay, but you won't have to put up with the cooing much longer. Mercedes is going to be transferring to Seattle shortly. How 'bout that?" I thought they were both going to hit the floor.

Since they were both speechless, I saw my opportunity to make my getaway. I headed toward the offices where Jay had said the victims were found.

"Hold on," Jay said. "You just can't leave us hanging out there in the breeze like that. Can you give us something a little more heavy? That's the ARRU-12 Team Lead position, right?"

It looked like someone had reached in and was squeezing Paul by the left lung. He was scared to take a breath.

"Don't look so surprised. What? Did y'all think this marriage of a team would last forever? I expect the same out of each and every one on this team. If you weren't striving for something bigger and better, I don't think I would even want you on my team. I expect—"

"This is not time for one of your lectures."

If I hadn't known better, I would have said Jay had a broken heart. Well, in Jay's case, more like a broken blood pump.

The distinctive simultaneous ring of tactical operations contacting the team gave me a nice distraction. "We're not done," I said.

I gave the rest of the team a second or two to make ready how they wanted to listen in, and then I gave operations the 'ARRU-7 online.'

I don't know why I was expecting some type of good news. Maybe because bad news had been humping my leg all day long and I figured it had to turn around sooner or later, but that wasn't the case.

It wasn't even a conversation. It was a recording telling us that we needed to drop whatever we were doing because of an elevated threat level.

The new leader, 'Salvo,' of the Firearm Freedom Brigade, had made it public knowledge via the media that plans had been set in motion to purify the voice of the Gun Control Advocacy.

Basically, they were about to go on a killing campaign of selected key elected officials and control advocates throughout the country. For some insane reason, they felt that if they could make the whole idea of gun control more costly than it was worth, it would simply go away.

The Bureau felt that this was a terrorism case; if it wasn't a terrorism case before, it sure was now. I felt in my gut that this was only the beginning, and I was already starting to miss Agrarian Mann.

Because of the limited resources, we were assigned babysitting duties for a couple of the officials in the area, at least until this new threat could be brought under control.

Mercedes came out of the office area, and it looked like she had made peace with whatever she had had going on with Mann.

Leslie popped her head in the door with a look of confusion. "So, we just drop the case all together?" she asked.

I looked at her, "Cases don't get dropped. They can be put on the back burner or placed on the shelf, but they never get dropped."

Mercedes rubbed the bridge of her nose. "Well, if we got everything, I suppose we don't need to waste any more time here."

Simultaneously, Jay said, "Yes, Sir," and Paul said, "Yes, Ma'am," and then they looked at each other and started a quiet private conversation.

"Isn't it still Ma'am?" Paul said. "I thought it was still Ma'am."

"Nah, they went back to gender neutral a couple years back. You're supposed to use 'Sir' for both male and female, at least in the ATF."

"Really, oh wow, isn't that something." Paul turned to Mercedes. "Sorry, Sir."

Somewhere, partially through their conversation, Mercedes's mouth had gone to full-on gapped open. She finally turned in my direction and threw those little fists on top of those hips.

"Damn it, Leslie," I said. "Outside, right now; let's run through it one more time." I had to turn her and hurry her along outside the building. She hadn't said so, but from her expression I take it that it was one of those things Mercedes wanted to announce herself.

This little diversion wouldn't stop her from blowing her top, but it would still be a nice stall.

CHAPTER 12 – NOT EVEN THE RITZ

I must admit, the Gun Control experiment is a failed project. Much like the bow and arrow, it's obvious that the only way these God forsaken relics will go away is to make them obsolete. Richard T. Thomas, noted Gun Control Advocate (2081)

It was almost sundown by the time we got back to the office, and the thought of giving myself a little something extra to keep me going was very tempting. It was the long days like this one that started to wear you down.

If he only knew what kind of mood I was in, the nightshift armorer sitting in my chair with his feet on top of my desk, would've probably taken cover.

The text message I received over the media device gave me the impression it was written in anger more than anything else. "The Director is waiting for you in conference room B." I was reading between the lines, of course.

"Thank you, Edith." It was already past Edith's normal work hours, and if you asked her to stay one minute pass her normal hours, well I'd compare it to poking a bear with a peppermint stick. It was just more trouble than it was worth.

"Sure, no problem. Now that I've delivered the message, I'm out of here," she replied.

The night MARRV Team was already getting comfortable for their twelve-hour shift. Still, they had their own desks so there was no excuse for any of them to be relaxing at any of ours.

I decided to go over and put it to him in a way to make sure that the guy had at least one or two really serious second thoughts about sitting at one of the desks again.

I grabbed the chair and spun it around, "Hey you—"

I was more surprised than the uniform. "What is this crap? What are you doing here, Nah? And what's with the get-up? I know you're still too young to be eligible to become an armorer, so what's going on?

Mercedes came up behind me and pushed me on the left side. "Move out of the way. I swear, sometimes it seems like you have no manners whatsoever. Hey, girl!" She threw her arms out to the sides and waited for an embrace.

Hannah stood and flashed a warm smile at me before she put her arms around Mercedes. "Hey, Merce, how you doing?"

"I'm doing great. It's always so nice to see you. Look at you; you look like a soldier." Mercedes released the embrace and held Hannah by the shoulders while she gave her a good look up and down.

"Yeah, well I'm still in school, but I decided to join the Cadet Corps." Hannah tilted her head in my direction. "Some people are always preaching and saying stuff like I could use some more self-discipline."

"Girl, just take it all with a grain of salt. Not everybody practices what they preach. Come on, we need to talk." Mercedes put her arm around her shoulders and started to lead her away.

"Uhh, excuse me," I said. They stopped and turned.

Mercedes continued her little rant while looking at me. "You don't want to keep the Director waiting, do you? We'll be here when you're done.

"Leslie, you want to join us?" Mercedes broke her gaze with me. "We're going over here to have a little girl talk."

"What about us?" Jay referred to himself and Paul. "Everything is supposed to be equal opportunity nowadays. We share the same restroom, for Christ's sake." He looked at me and continued with his little comment, "Damned mirror hogs."

I shook my head and turned to Mercedes's direction, "Don't be poisoning my daughter with that evil girl gossip." Without taking my eyes off the ladies, I said to Jay and Paul, "I see I need to get in there and get out as soon as possible."

Paul shook his head and closed his eyes before adding his two cents, "Why do I get the feeling that if the walls had ears, in a couple of minutes they would start bleeding?"

I hoped it wasn't that bad, but I found myself agreeing with the whole concept.

I headed over to the conference room and found the Director along with his executive assistant in the throes of an e-documentation review.

"Ah, come on in, Harris. Have a seat."

They continued to flip through eDocs for another half a minute or so. I guess he didn't know how valuable my time was. The poisoning of a young impressionable mind was in progress, and I had to make sure it didn't get out of hand.

"Sorry to pull you off your case, but this new assignment has the highest priority. My thinking is the people I'm responsible to are terrified that if we fail to provide adequate protection to the Advocates of the Gun Control Act, it would somehow be directly linked to the Wreck and Wrap project. They would like to avoid giving the joint task force a black eye."

"I understand," I said. "Everybody's resources are thin and even though it'll be tough, I don't mind covering the gaps; at least as much as we can."

"Great. As you are well aware, there is a summit scheduled for next Tuesday. Five of the speakers are flying in tomorrow morning. The Bureau is taking Senator Able, Doctor Samantha Stapleton, and Doctor Barry Elder. They asked if we could cover Mister Mark Wilson and the Reverend Phil Tomkins."

The Reverend Phil Tomkins—well wasn't that just dandy. It figured we would get the most outspoken, and from what I'd heard, the most egotistical of the whole bunch. No big surprise there. We got him because the Bureau didn't want him. *A job's a job, I guess.*

The Executive Assistant started typing away at her keyboard again, and then I heard a tone from my phone.

"That would be their itineraries," he said.

I pulled up the document to give it the once over. "Nothing here tells me how long this assignment is."

The Director nodded. "I understand; nothing I have suggests how long this assignment will be."

He must've known this was unacceptable for me. "Every project has a definite start date and a definite end date. This is not our primary function, so I'd like to have some idea—"

"You guys can return to the full and undivided attention of your investigations after the summit," he said. "The recommendation was for someone to provide twenty-four/seven including travel. It wasn't easy, but I got permission for a review of the situation after the summit. I'll stall until you get back into the field. After the review, whatever the outcome it will be at least several days before I can catch up with you. Right now that's the best I can do."

I stood up. "Thank you, Sir. The sooner we get back on it, the sooner such assignments won't be necessary."

He made a nod of agreement.

I turned to leave.

"Just so you know," the Director said, "we'll be out of your hair tomorrow. The Bureau Chief and the others are already gone. We'll be on our way back to Washington by 9 am, so you can have your cars back. I'm sure you want to give the rollers a break." I think it was the first time I had seen him smile since he had been here, but his assistant gave a little laugh out loud. "Pardon the pun."

I think I was more in shock from the dryness of the humor than anything else. Geez, break… roller. The joke was pretty bad, but I gave him a nasal laugh for the effort.

"You know," he said. "I was hoping to catch one of your renowned analogies I have heard so much about. Maybe next time."

Ahh, so it all comes to light. The Associate Deputy Director has been talking about me.

"Oh sure, Sir, I'll come up with something for you next time, but with respect to sitting on Reverend Tomkins, I'm not sure which one I would like more: this assignment or an infected herpie on a hemorrhoid."

"Yep," he said. "I think that one will do it. I think I've reached my analogy quota. Don't worry about next time."

When I got back out into the main office area, my team was nowhere to be found. I forwarded the assignment and itineraries I had just gotten and waited for it.

The moans and groans from conference room 'C' were almost in unison. I walked over and opened the door, and there they all were, hogging what little quality-time I had with my daughter. I guess I couldn't complain. Since Paul and Jay were in there, they couldn't dedicate their time to strictly girl talk.

Jay held up his phone with the document on it. "This is fuc—" he cut his eyes over in Hannah's direction. "This is messed up. How come we get the two biggest… pains in the neck?"

I had to laugh at him, simply because I knew he didn't really care. "Well, we weren't around for first picks, so it is what it is."

"Oh is that how it is, huh? If that's the case, Paul and I can pick up the billionaire Mark Wilson."

"Hey," Mercedes didn't shout, but it was a bit louder than her moan and groan.

"I think I'm going to share the dividing up of chores of this one with the Seattle Boss."

Mercedes crossed her arms and nodded. "Since he is known to be such a handful, Jay and Kyle, you two guys take Reverend Tomkins. It's well known that Mark Wilson travels with his own entourage, so we don't need to serve up a bunch of our own resources there. Paul can cover him by himself.

"Leslie and I can review the image-set and continue the investigation while the leads are still hot."

I looked back over to Jay, "See. Now that's how it's done. Insightful and without hesitation; we'll all be working for Associate Director Molina one day."

Jay slapped his forehead, "Dear Lord, say it isn't so."

"What's all this talk about Seattle?" Hannah asked.

Merce smiled. "I've received an appointment as the new Team Lead in the field office up there."

Hannah's jaw dropped, and then she looked at me.

"Well we have our assignments," I said. "I won't get my vehicle back until after 9 am, so Jay, I'll need for you to pick me up at 7 tomorrow morning to catch that 8:15 arrival from Chicago.

Jay stood, "Yeah, yeah," and then made his way over to Hannah and gave her a hug. "How long you gonna be in town, Nah?"

"I'm just home for the weekend."

"It's obvious that other folks don't care that your Dad might wanna spend some time with you this weekend," Jay looked over at Mercedes, "but I'll figure out a way we can get him away and get a break from the good Reverend."

"Oh, don't even try it," Mercedes said. "Anyway, I guess you're going to be staying at your Dad's place while you're here?"

"Sounds like he is going to be out most of the weekend, so I'm going to say my bags will be there. I'm not going to stay there and visit with the cat. I'll be in and out, but you have my contact info."

"Sorry, honey, you caught me at a bad time."

"Uh huh, same ole' song; you could at lease use a different tune," she said.

Leslie laughed out loud. "Oh my goodness! Not only does she look like you, she sounds like you too."

Jay started moving toward the door. "Yeah, well, we're still trying to break her from that. Alright, I hate to make a break, but there are a couple of things I have to take care of because I'm expecting a long day tomorrow."

Hannah gave him a nod of understanding. "See ya, Uncle Jay."

Jay paused and flashed that crooked smile. "I'll see you again before you go." He swung the door open, made his exit, and allowed the door to close on its own.

"Yeah, it's kind of late." Paul stood and stretched his back. "Merce, sorry to be rude, but you're hogging what little time they could be having together... and don't give me that I love her like a daughter stuff. Time to go."

It probably took quite a bit of restraint for Mercedes not to give one of her sharp rebuttals; she just looked at Paul for a moment and then rolled her eyes in some type of hated agreement.

"I'll call you, Nah."

"If you don't, I'll call you," she replied.

The sound of the door closing behind them left me with mixed feelings. My brain was working overtime on all the things that were happening. They all seemed to be moving so fast, you'd swear they were riding the tail end of a whip.

Hannah was a new variable that I could now throw into the mix. There was no way I could neglect this opportunity. Since she had gotten back in school, I typically only saw her on the weekends, but it was not uncommon to not see her for several months. There was only one thing to do. Be the loving, caring, and patient parent I had always been.

"What in the hell is with this Cadet Corps crap? I thought you said that you wouldn't ever become an agent."

"How can you work with women and know so little about them?" she said. "We always have a right to change our minds. Besides, this is just the Cadet Corps. How do you know I don't wanna go to the Bureau after I graduate."

"Oh dear Lord, heaven help us all," I said.

****

Jay was running a bit late the next morning. Fortunately, I could track his media device, and he was just a couple minutes away. Still plenty of time to make it to the airport and have an overpriced burger or something.

Moments later, I heard the bawling of tires on the smooth pavement of the garage.

The car never came to a complete stop, but it did come to a roll slow enough for me to open the door and jump in.

"Do you have any idea how dangerous that is? You couldn't come to a complete stop?"

He just laughed at my question. "Well you should be happy you have a car to jump in. You could be in the same boat as Mercedes and stuck with a roller."

That comment came as a surprise, but I was more curious than anything else. "What do you mean stuck?"

"Someone came in early and sent all the available vehicles to the motor pool for safety violations. Oh, with the exception of Paul's vehicle, of course."

"Are you trying to win the asshole of the month award?" I asked.

"I'm not saying it was me. Who knows, maybe it was one of those big dawgs that was in town. They were the ones that had all the cars. Maybe the cars just weren't up to their Washington D.C. standards."

I considered the beauty of it. "In any case, once a safety violation has been reported on a vehicle, it's down until it passes a complete diagnostics. That was a pretty good one. A low-down, evil, dirty trick, but a good one. They probably won't even get started on a vehicle until about 9 am, and it will most likely be unavailable all day. The thought of what would be the expression on Mercedes face made me burst-out in laughter. "Yep, that certainly is asshole of the month material."

The ride to the airport was kind of peaceful. Oh sure, Jay went on and on about how this crappy assignment would cramp his style with the new girl he just met; but, since there was always a new girl, I figured she was just another flavor of the month.

We arrived with plenty of time to spare. I even had time to have a sit-down with my breakfast burger; unfortunately, the peace and tranquility of my morning meal was interrupted by Mercedes wondering what happened to all the vehicles and if there was something I could do. It didn't help much when I told her she would probably look really hot in a spin-suit.

Out of curiosity, I checked Paul's location, and it showed him about 100 feet away. One guy appeared wearing the signature enhanced surveillance eyewear—or E.S.E. eyes—of a bodyguard; although he was dressed like a tourist, it was obvious what his real role was. He took up position on the far wall and surveyed the area. He made a few comments to his fist while another—and I could've almost sworn clone of himself—walked by.

Jay leaned back, folded his arms, and then shook his head. "When are we going to get some of those fancy E.S.E. eyeballs?"

"Not in the budget buddy," I said. "Not this year, or the next."

The well-to-do Mark Wilson appeared with several other people along with Paul. Just like we knew where Paul was, I guess he had the same idea. He looked over at us with his brand new set of E.S.E., smiled, and then gave us the thumbs up.

"You need to put down the time he spends with that detail as vacation time," Jay said.

"That is a pretty tempting idea."

They disappeared down the corridor, and then finally the first guy did a quick survey of the rear before he tried to play catch up.

Jay looked over in my direction. "Alright, don't get any ideas. We are both too old to be playing leapfrog."

"Shoot, never crossed my mind. Besides, we would need at least four more knuckleheads on this detail."

It was another thirty minutes before the Reverend Tomkins's plane arrived. Jay hung back in the lobby area, but I decided to meet him at the aircraft door just in case one of the aircraft support personnel was a little shady.

The cabin crew was kind enough to let the VIPs exit the plane first. At least they pretended it was kindness. I'm sure it was policy since other VIPs followed.

This was the first time I had seen him in person, but he was unmistakable. Tall and large, he looked like a man who could hold his own. He was built a lot like Jay. I showed him my badge.

"How you doing there, Reverend? My name is—"

"You're not one of those Serendipitan people are you? I can't have any of those Serendipitan people creeping around me." Yep, built a lot like Jay and just as loud; I prayed that this wouldn't turn into a head butting session.

"No, Reverend, I'm not a member of the Serendipitan faith, and I can assure you that no member of my team is. Now, I don't have the details of how many people are in your party. If we could just—"

"Oh, thank the Lord Jesus," he said. "I can handle any of the other religions, even most of the new fake ones. But, that one just doesn't pass the test. You have to believe in the Lord. You can call him any name you want, but his name is not destiny. You know what I mean?"

Yeah, I knew what he meant. He meant to let me know that he wanted to be in control of this relationship, and that was going to make my job a lot harder. It was going to be a long day.

I finally got him and his assistant out into the lobby, but the first thing on his agenda was to size Jay up. I reckon he was always used to being the biggest guy in the room. The fact that Jay was just as big as he was seemed to tamper with his confidence.

"We've made arrangements for you at an undisclosed location that I'm told meet your requirements," I said. His assistant looked shocked, and then I heard him whisper.

"Philly, you know I only do the Ritz. I've already made the reservations."

Yep, the rumors were true about the Reverend. His assistant didn't come across as a Gay-boy, but it was pretty obvious.

The Reverend turned to us. "Well, I want you to know I appreciate everything you're doing for us, but to allow these threats to change how I live my life is the same as letting them win. They will not win. I have something more powerful than they could possibly imagine on my side. I have plans and scheduled meetings, so I must insist on the Ritz-Richardson."

I looked at Jay. He shrugged, smiled, and said, "I could do the Ritz." Lot of help he was.

We finally made our way to the secured area where we parked the car and the assistant started in again.

"This is not a limousine; Philly, you know I only ride in a limo and this—" Jay opened the door to the back seat before he could finish.

"Man, get your ass in the car." The expression on Jay's face said he was about fed up. I kind of wanted to see how it played out so I didn't interfere.

As expected, the Reverend stepped forward, flexing and barking. "Okay, let's get one thing straight, I will not, nor any of my people will be disrespected in any way. Do we understand each other?"

Time seemed to freeze for a moment. The only movement came from a flick of Jay's wrist. The car door closed.

About three seconds after the door closed, Jay stood tall, stepped towards the Reverend, and put his hands on his waist.

"You're absolutely right. I was out of line, and that was very unprofessional of me." Jay was very calm, and the sound of his voice was almost apologetic—almost. The Reverend stood with his chest pushed out so far that I thought he was going to break his own back.

Jay walked around the Reverend and stood between him and his assistant. He turned to the assistant and kept his back to the Reverend. Jay's comment was slow and steady.

"I need you to help me keep the both of you safe. It is very, very important that I have your full cooperation." I couldn't see Jay's face, but I could imagine the expression.

Five seconds later the guy pursed his lips, rolled his eyes, walked over to the car door, and then turned his back to all of us. Jay looked over to me and raised his eyebrows. I had to admit, I was starting to have a ball.

Jay walked over and opened the car door. The assistant got in without another word.

The Reverend walked around to the other door, and before he got in he commented to Jay, "You know an actual apology wouldn't hurt."

"Well, Reverend, you're in the business of saving people's souls, so you're probably a whole lot better at it than me. Right now, I'm in the business of risking the life my mother was so kind enough to give me to protect you and yours. I will not have anyone apologize to her because I was apologetic. What I mean is that no one is going to be telling my mother 'Sorry for the loss of your son' because I needed to tell people I was sorry."

After the Reverend got into the car, I was free to flash my pearly-whites at Jay. He shook his head and headed to the passenger side. "You drive," he said. "I'm feeling a little stressed."

For some reason, the good Reverend felt the need to enlighten us on his mission in life along the way to the Ritz. Attempting to be a good host, I pretended to listen to his stories of self-glorification, but I was more focused on scanning the landscape for possible threats. I looked to my right, and Jay was sitting quiet and focused. It was at that point that I noticed he was holding his snag. It lay in his lap, green light at the ready.

At that point, just for a second, I was more worried about the assistant than an attack by the FFB.

"Doesn't hurt to be ready," he said. The truth was, Jay would more likely pull the BISCIT from the trunk and put the guy in a mechanically induce coma. That wasn't a concern either, because once I stopped the car, if I thought he was about to do that, I could simply drive off when he made his way around to the trunk.

I was glad to finally make it to the hotel. Even though it was doubtful, there was a possibility that once he got in his room, the Reverend would shut the hell up.

As soon as we pulled up into the driveway, a valet was already out to make us welcome. Jay had his door open and his foot out before the car came to a complete stop.

"I got it," he said to the young man before he could grab the door handle.

Another was making his way around to the driver's side to park the car. I opened the car door and tapped on my badge hanging from my shirt.

"Sorry, son, you won't be able to drive this vehicle unless you have genetic material stored in the Federal Agent Authorization Database. I'm going to need for you to step back." As the breath left his body, it looked like he lost two pounds. "I'm going to need to leave this vehicle here until we can get our passengers checked-in and secure in their room."

He stopped, held his hands in the air, palms facing out. "Yes, sir, no problem."

I would have appreciated it if the Rev and his friend would have hurried, but they decided to mosey along like they were walking the red carpet. The Reverend smile, waved, and reveled in the light of a celebrity.

This whole thing gave me an uneasy feeling. It would have been so nice to conduct a little bit of monitoring before the actual transport. Not really a necessity, but it would have made it a lot easier to pick out the things that seemed out of place.

Fortunately, it was still early in the day, and you wouldn't expect the hotel to be a hive of activity, not even the Ritz.

I made mental notes on the way to the counter: elderly couple lounging in the lobby. Across the room in the bar, two middle-aged business men having a nooner. Young girl, probably sixteen or seventeen, behind the counter. I scanned the walls and inside the huge planters and vases for devices. So far, everything looked just grand. I would have to come take a second look after they were secure.

As we approached the counter, around the corner, by the elevator there was an elderly woman arguing with who I assumed to be an Assistant Manager. Not something I could consider out of place.

Five paces from the counter, I grabbed Reverend Tomkins by the shoulder. "Why don't you hang back here with me," I said and pointed to his assistant. "You, go ahead and get the room." A look of terror swept over him. He started looking around.

"Is there something wrong?" he asked.

"Nope, everything's sweet; we don't need everyone pinned up against the counter."

"But why me? Why can't—"

"You made the reservation, so you get the room." He turned and looked at the Reverend. "Kid, try to relax," I said. "You're only getting a hotel room."

The Reverend tried to ease his fears. "Go get the room, Jason. You know the one I like." The kid made a fearful smile but now had the motivation to make a move for the check-in counter.

When the kid reached the counter, the whole world suddenly seemed to change. The elderly lady at the elevator with the manager were now whispering and eyeing us out of the corner of their eye. The two men at the bar had moved to a table next to the lobby. The elderly couple lounging and watching the media circuit were gone.

I heard Jay over my earpiece, "I got 'em; they are in the east hall. You're looking for the two old folks that were watching the circuit, right?" I looked and there they were, holding hands like they were in love. That was too much for me. "Reverend, let's back off a bit. Tell you what, let's move over to—"

The receptionist tried to get the Reverend's attention. "Reverend Tomkins, I'm sorry and I don't mean to bother you, but I was really hoping to get an autograph."

"Now, see, how could I refuse a smile like that?" I could tell the Rev had his 'they love me' face on.

"Something is not right, so I'm going to have to insist," I said, but the Reverend being who he was, decided he needed to argue with me.

"Anytime someone wants to share their love of the faith with me, especially a young person, I'm going to—"

"RELICS!" I saw the two at the bar pop-up out of their chairs with handgun-class relics, but I think both Jay and I shouted the alarm at the same time.

I didn't have time for the Reverend's crap, and since I felt he wasn't the type to hit the ground and take cover with any enthusiasm, I planted my shoulder in his gut, grabbed him behind the kneecaps, and then gave him a good push and pull.

"Oh, my hip!" he shouted.

I should have been the one complaining. That was probably about two hundred and thirty pounds on my lower back.

We landed on the floor, in a nest of tables and chairs. Although the small tables wouldn't offer much cover, I kicked them over around the Reverend to at least give him some added protection until the situation was under control.

Thankfully, I was fast enough to get the Reverend on the ground before they could engage us, and Jay was now in a fire fight with the two. He had good cover, so I took a quick look around for additional threats. Jason and the young receptionist were both gawking with their mouths open.

"You two, get down!" I shouted

Jason squatted where he stood and cover his head with his forearms. The girl disappeared behind the counter.

Before I could give Jay a hand, both the manager and the old lady with the room complaints came running around the corner; both of them shooting wildly with one hand. Table chips were flying in every direction, and they probably would have had me if they had taken their time.

Alright, prone or sitting? I chose sitting so I could look over the table tops.

I spun on my hip to a sitting position, drew my knees up, and planted my elbows on the inside of my knees. I had to give a 'hooray' to the training, because it was all simultaneous. My elbows landed on the insides of my knees, the butt of the snag dropped and steadied in my free hand. The old lady dropped like someone had ripped out her spine.

The snipers would have been proud of me; it was one shot, one kill. She lay there on her back with knees pushed forward. She looked like she was getting ready to limbo.

"Mom? Momma?" I didn't have time to feel sorry for the guy, and his trauma was the opening I needed.

The double tap center mass dropped him, and he clutched his chest while he made an attempt to crawl away. He made it three feet, gasping for air, before he expired.

Now I had the opportunity to give my focus to the remaining threat in the bar area. I made another butt spin to change the angle of my seated position, but I couldn't get a lock on any of the assailants. I heard the weapons fire, but I couldn't see them from the cover they had taken.

The whole room lit up from the flash of the F.I.D., and it was obvious they knew the advantage had shifted because one of them tried to make a run for it. The other, in desperation, stood up and shot blindly. I don't think he cared what he hit, as long as he hit something.

The round Jay laid in the chest caused him to backpedal and fall partially through the partition separating the lobby from the bar.

After the one that tried to make a run for it slammed into the lobby wall, I just stood to get a clear shot.

"Drop your weapons," I said.

He did, but it didn't stop him from trying to make a run for it. I put a round in the left buttock. The way he was screaming, you would've thought someone had taken a horsewhip to him.

"You got him, Jay?"

He was moving toward him, but we were both still scanning the area for other threats.

"Yeah, I got him. Are we secure?"

"Looks like it's all clear," I said.

"Jason?" The Reverend rolled to his hands and knees.

His assistant was still crouched in a ball against the check-in counter and was locked in a chant. "Oh Lord, oh Jesus, praise his name, praise his name…"

The Reverend jumped to his feet and made a dash for his assistant.

"Reverend Tomkins!" I said. "You need to stay with me."

Not unexpectedly, my commands fell on deaf ears. He reached down for his assistant and pulled him up. He first checked him for any bullet holes and then he held him by the cheeks and attempted to comfort him. "Everything is going to be alright," he said. "You're okay; it's over."

The receptionist finally rose from behind the counter. She looked at the damage we had done and covered her mouth while her eyes shifted from one body to another.

"Miss, I need for you to call an emergency crew," I said.

Her eyes continued to shift through the devastation.

"Miss? I really need for you to…" I recognized the look. It wasn't trauma; in fact, I was more traumatized than she was. The expression underneath the hand that covered that mouth was rage.

There was no need to chamber the round; the weapon was already loaded. The proximity of the weapon from Tomkins's face was probably the biggest factor. If it had been a long barrel, it would have taken his head completely off; however, the short barrel of the shotgun was still effective enough. The double-aught buck lifted all two-hundred and thirty pounds off the ground and peeled his face right off.

The girl—still with the look of rage—threw the weapon over the counter, put her hands on top of her head and looked at me. I dropped my weapon to my side and shook my head.

I wanted to blame the Reverend for being so hard-headed, but no matter what the case was, in the end, I had failed.

Jason's gaze was locked on Tomkins, but I guess it finally sunk in, and he fainted very gracefully, spinning like a top while he made some kind of ballerina fall to the ground.

I suppose the curiosity got the best of the girl. She had to look over the counter and down to see the damage she had done. What was left of old Phil Tomkins wasn't for the weak, and she immediately blew chunks all over the hardwood. At the same time she bent over to release the contents of her stomach, I was over the counter to make sure there was nothing else behind the bar.

I held onto the back of her shirt, but pointed my weapon at the two nosy valets coming in to see what the commotion was all about.

"You two, sit down over there." They did, and they sat there quietly with their hands head high.

"What the heck is going on?" one asked.

"And be quiet," I added. I returned my attention to the girl. "You have any more friends around here?" The clink of the handcuffs was the sound of her young life fading away.

"You killed all my friends, you bastard."

"Jay, made a quick sweep and kept it tight."

He nodded and brought over the guy with the shot in the butt and had him lay against the check-in counter.

I brought the girl around and sat her down next to him. I had to comment about how long it took him to get control of the two behind the bar. "I can't believe those two gave you all that trouble. You must be getting slow in your old age."

"It was the bartender that was a booger-bear," he said. "I know you couldn't see him from your position, but he was dug in there pretty deep." He moved to begin his search.

I got on the phone and called for the works. I needed an emergency team, a MAARV Unit, and I had to let the local PD know. I was still on the phone when Jay came back with his weapons drawn, moving fast in a crouched tactical position.

"Where'd they go?" he asked.

"Who?"

"The valets; Seven employees were locked up in a storeroom back there. Two of them were valets.

The valets were gone. The only thing left of them was the memory of them holding their hands in the air. I searched my mind for some way out, some clever comeback that would allow me to save face. After a moment of pondering, I had it, and I was ready to make it right.

"Well now, ain't I the monkey's uncle."

What else could I say?

CHAPTER 13 – STILL ONE OF MY FAVORITES

There are many roads to success. Ours is a straight line. Do not stress that other zigzag through a life of confusion. Eventually, they will cross your path and see your light at the top of the hill. You shall lead the way. Book of Serendipitan Values, Chapter 3 (2077)

The dissension in the ranks was starting to become a major irritation for me. Even though the details of my little coup were still a mystery to the members of the organization as a whole, mystery or not, I felt the challenge to my leadership brewing. The sounds of a pair of feet running down the hall fueled my paranoia and did nothing for my peace of mind.

"Salvo, I think you're going to want to take this call." My new lieutenant stood at the door holding out the phone.

I waved him in and wondered if I had appointed this new lieutenant in haste. I needed people with balls, but he acted like he had broken glass in his boots the way he walked in. I could sense the fear when I took the phone from him.

"I've been getting nothing but bad news all day." Both of the targets, Mark Wilson and Juan Chavez, had failed. "Steel, I swear, if you guys weren't so expensive…"

Lady Hammer stepped into the doorway. That damned Melody Jenson was here; I knew she was out on bail, but I didn't know she had caught up with us.

"Yes, the contractors are expensive, but they aren't nearly as expensive as what we've experience from the loss of life with these half-baked schemes of yours." she said. "We are a militia, and the truth of the matter is our people have had a limited about of tactical training. Nothing near the level of training of the people you've put them against."

I chose to ignore her for the moment and returned my attention to the incoming phone call. "So, do you have any idea what this is about? My guess is the Target Phil Tomkins project, would that be about right?"

"Well, yeah, but I thought you would want—"

I took the phone from him. "Just give me the status," I said and put the thing on top of the desk.

He mumbled, "Well, they were successful with the target, but most of the people—our people— were killed. The two scouts assigned to make the initial contact got away, but Lil Red and Singer were captured."

I felt the pressure behind my eyes building. My thumb and index finger did little to offer relief. "See," I said. "That wasn't so hard."

The phone shattered into more fragments than I could count after it hit the wall. Everyone—with the exception of Steel—ducked.

"Everyone out and pack it up. We're moving to a new base of operations. Have everyone ready to go in an hour."

Steel remained in his chair, and Melody stood in the doorway with hate and contempt in her eyes, but she finally left also.

"Her and that Lenard Anderson are going to be a problem," I said.

Steel laughed. "You know what I always say: there's no such thing as a problem, only the absence of a solution. You've got to stay positive."

The sound of the doorbell sent everyone scrambling. I made my way to the living room, where I found everyone loading weapons and taking up positions.

"You people need to calm yourselves," I said.

The new lieutenant whispered in a panic, "It's the ATF; they found us."

I checked the security monitor, and there on the screen was Special Agent Mercedes Molina, all sparkly in a shiny spin-suit.

"Relax," I said. "If they found us, they wouldn't be knocking, or in this case, ringing the doorbell." The doorbell rang again, and I thought a couple people were going to lose their stomachs. I tried to pick out the calmest person in the group;

unfortunately, the calmest person was Steel. "I can't get the door; she knows me. Do you mind getting the door?"

"Oh, not at all." Steel looked himself over and tried to make himself look as domestic as possible. What a waste of time. Not even close; it wasn't possible. "I don't think she paid much attention to me," he said, "but, let's just hope she doesn't remember me from the hospital, when I went to pick up Agrarian."

I went back over to the security monitor and turned on the audio, since I was very curious why and how they knew to come here.

The past couple of days had been really hot and today was no different, but the fresh air that came through the front door gave me a chill.

"Oh, hello, officer. How can I help you?"

"Good morning, sir. Sorry to bother you. We were just following up on some leads on a recent incident that resulted in the deaths of several individuals. I was wondering if we could come in and have a word with you. It should only be a few moments of your time."

"Gee, officer, I can't imagine how I could be of assistance. What are you looking for? Maybe I've seen it around."

I noticed her move to the side and try to look around him and make something between a comment and a question, "You're not going to let me in are you?"

"To be honest with you, officer, I have no authority to do that. I'm just a guest of the house."

"Uh, huh," she said and continued scrolling through her phone. "So you're not Jeremy Mills?"

"Who?"

"Jeremy Mills, the owner."

He paused for a moment. "You know, I can't tell you if that is the owner's actual name or not. I was invited by a friend of the owner. Just out of curiosity, what makes you think that someone associated with this address could be connected with this... incident you said? The one that resulted in the death of several individuals."

"One of the victims was wearing an arm brace. The serial number associated with the purchase of the brace was not associated with this address; however, other purchases by the company that purchased the one he was wearing are."

"I'm shocked. Well, ain't that a dingle-berry."

"Uh, huh. Well, there is nothing free in this old world," Agent Molina said. "People will always leave some type of money trail. You'd have to be a real pro to know how to hide that. Do you have any idea when the owner will be back? I only ask so I know how much time I'll need to get the warrant."

Steel shrugged and smiled. "I would imagine they'll be back at any moment."

"Oh, really," she said. "Okay, well then, we'll just wait out here. It's such a nice day. Thanks for your help."

"Sure, I just wish I could've been more of assistance," he said.

Agent Molina had made it halfway across the yard where she met up with her partner before the my contractor gave her pause. "Now that I think about it," he added.

She stopped, turned her shoulder toward him, and gave him an over-the-shoulder look.

"They did tell me not to wait up, so actually it could be several hours."

She gave no response. She turned and continued walking. The other, new agent refused to take her eyes off the house. Instead, she took a few steps backward, turned and walked at an angle still never taking her eyes off the house or Steel.

They both climbed into their rollers and fired up the engines. The exhale in the room was pretty loud after they took off.

Steel came over and whispered to me, "We need to get out of here."

"Right," I said. "Everyone get ready to move. Load up the—"

"No, I mean right now." The sweat on Steel's face was a little more than the result of a hot day. "Look," he continued. "I don't work for these other swinging dicks, I work for you. Those fancy souped-up vehicles they're riding can see through walls. The only reason they didn't use the feature is because unreasonable search and privacy laws won't allow them to ride up to the house and start scanning. At least, not until they have a reasonable amount of suspicion. Not to mention they had to travel at a relatively slow pace through the city and the residential streets to get to the house, so I'm pretty sure their batteries are low.

"Me not letting them in was enough to make them reasonably suspicious, and since they took off down the street a whole lot faster than they need too, the only reason I can think of for that is that they needed a little gusto to charge the batteries cells. My guess is we have about ten to fifteen minutes before they are back to scan the house, so we need to beat feet."

"Salvo, I need to have a word with you." Melody stepped up to me like she was ready to make her stand.

"We don't have time for this right now, Lady Hammer."

"We'll have to make time because your recklessness has brought just about everything we've worked for to its knees. All our plans—"

"All your plans went south," I said, "when your Commander decided to go homicidal on your beloved Council. You should be thanking me for stopping him. But, this is a discussion for another day. Right now, we have to go."

We didn't have ten to fifteen. The rollers coming to a sliding stop gave their return away. The two ARRU agents were back, but this time the noses of their vehicles were pointed directly at the house. Since the bulk of the people in the house were still scampering about with that look of relief on their faces, carrying their weapons and waving them in the air, I can only imagine what the agents saw on their screens.

"I want everyone that can fit loaded into the van and ready to move on my signal… you have twenty seconds." The dumb-asses stopped their celebrating and looked at me. "You now have fifteen, so MOVE IT."

Everyone started scrambling for the garage.

"Not you, Melody. We'll be able to get away, but I need your help here." I walked over to the security panel and held up my media device. "Ray, I'll let you know when to go. Don't go until I tell you to do so."

"Got it!" he said.

I turned back to the panel and prepped the emergency evacuation procedure.

"What do you need me to do?" Melody asked.

I held up my left index finger. I needed just a moment to focus. Would they take the bait? Only one did. One of the rollers spun out and headed to block the garage exit. It would have to do.

In the driveway, just inches below her wheels, stuffed into one inch diameter metal tubing, lay about forty feet of detonation cord.

As soon as the vehicle entered the driveway, I threw the switch to arm the primer and then punched the button for zone one to set off the trap.

"Okay, Melody, this is what I need for you to do."

The blade entered her right eye. Her entire body became stiff and rigid. I was sure the blade had pierced her brain, but I didn't have time to enjoy it and wait for her to slowly die; I had things to do.

I grabbed her by the hair at the base of the skull, used my hip for leverage, and pulled her down to the ground. Once on the ground, I put my knee on top of her chest and rotated the wrist of my knife hand clockwise in large circles. She had a beautiful eye socket. It made a perfect pivot point.

Steel crossed his arms, shook his head, and then laughed. "Scrambled eggs, huh? Man, I haven't seen you do that since the VA project."

"Yeah," I ripped my blade from her skull. "Still one of my favorites, though." Her blouse really sucked at cleaning the blade, so I used the bottom of one of her pant legs instead.

I went back to the security monitors but couldn't see anything for the smoke and dust.

"If you're looking for the second roller," he said while looking out a side window. "She has gone to help the one you blew bouncing like a cue ball on a bad break."

"Well, that'll be the bad break we need." I grabbed my media device. "Ray, now would be the time to make a break for it."

"We are outta here," came back over the phone.

I knew my time might be coming to an end. I could stall them, but I knew eventually a genetics team would get in here, and if they were successful in finding any genetics, unlike most of my counterparts like Steel, my information can be found in the national database.

I set the remaining charges to cover our escape. It would be several weeks before they would be able to get in. The entire house was laced with lithium and magnesium to convert the ground it lay on into a delta fire. They could wish it, they could want it, they could even piss on it, but it didn't matter; they didn't have anything that could put out a delta fire. I am the Salvo.

"Salvo, we can't get out. The door is jammed; the explosion jammed the door!" This new lieutenant sounded frantic. If he only knew that he had more reason than a jammed door to be worried about.

"Ray, you're fired. Look, blow the hinges, ram the door with the car, do whatever you have to do to get those people to the next safe house. There will not be an explosion, but in less than two minutes this house is going to start a long slow burn until it reaches about 5,000 degrees. You don't want to be here when that happens." I shut off the device.

"You ready to go?" Steel stood next to the bar that he had moved to expose the set of tunnels we needed to make our escape.

"Sure, why not," I said. "I don't really have a lot of fond memories of this place, and I could use a change of venue."

They had to be monitoring the movement sensors in the tunnel since they were waiting for us on the other side. Dank and dirty down there, but the tunnels weren't meant to be comfortable.

I popped my head out of the tunnel entrance. "Did they make it out of the garage?"

"Yes sir, and the way they took off you would've thought the devil was coming for their souls."

"Good. What's our current situation?"

He leaned over and made a little peep out the window. "We have a lookout getting the status right now."

I looked out the window and saw one of our oldest members—Carol something, I forget—out there in a housecoat playing the nosy neighbor role. She was asking the agents if they needed any help.

Since the one standing was the new agent, I had to assume the one flat on her back was Agent Molina. Too bad, I had always liked Molina. Oh well, it's a dangerous world we live in.

"I hear you're looking for a new lieutenant?"

I didn't know this young upstart asking the question, but you had to admire the ambition. I had already made one mistake with a hasty appointment of a lieutenant; I wasn't about to make another.

"We'll talk," I said.

Mistakes, so many mistakes; we couldn't afford any more. At every turn, somebody wants to shoot holes in my plans. If not the ARRU, then it's someone in my own organization. It first started with that damned council, and I doubt it will end with Melody Jenson.

They should thank me. They should be thanking me and cheering my name.

They would have never come close to what I'd achieved with their passive agenda. They needed something more radical, and I'd brought the gamma ray burst that left the ground smoldering in my wake everywhere I went.

There would be casualties on both sides, and that was unfortunate, but seeing the smoke billowing from the carnage outside filled me with a new level of excitement.

I was just getting started.

CHAPTER 14 – I'M ONE OF THE GOOD GUYS

To be honest, I'm comfortable with either a relic or a snag. I'm not bias and neither is death. From a legal standpoint, I'm just here to clean up the mess. Reginald Pendergrass, Bar-None Public Affairs Officer (2093)

Mercedes was down. The whole concept left this cold feeling inside of me. After I heard the news, as much as I hated it, I had to see the playback from the roller she was in.

It showed the roller turning toward the house and silhouettes bouncing all over the place with what were either snags or relics. I saw her heading for a garage door at breakneck speed, and then smoke.

Even though they told me she was down, I knew in my heart she was okay. I just hadn't seen it with my own eyes, or knew it in my mind yet. What I had seen in my brain brought back recent memories of my own fiasco in the roller, and both Leslie and I walked away with a couple of scratches and some minor bumps and bruises.

I wanted to rush to the scene and play the role of the distraught boyfriend, but since the MARRV had just arrive to secure the area, we had no choice but to wait on scene until they checked inventory and secured all the relics. It was just policy and procedural stuff.

By the time they gave us the word that they were secure, I finally received the incoming call. I guess Leslie finally got a grip on the situation and slowed down enough to give us a call.

"What's going on, Les? How's Mercedes?"

"Well, I guess she's okay. Right now, she's threatening to put one of the EMTs through a windshield if he doesn't clear her for full active duty."

I overheard a lot of fussing in the background, but not enough to make sense of it.

"Put her on the phone. On second thought, if you ask her to take the phone, she'll tell you to piss off, so just put your phone up to her ear and wait for a nod." I could tell she was walking toward Mercedes because the fussing was getting louder and clearer.

"Sure thing, boss," she said. I listened and waited for the breath… ah, there. There was the signature huff and puff of Mercedes.

"Hey, asshole, there is one and one way only that you are going to be cleared for full duty and that is after a full physical examination and anything they say that they think MIGHT be required to make sure there is no hidden head trauma; so you're going to sit there and behave yourself, now stop acting like a brain-damaged child and let them finish what they have to do.

"If the EMTs decide to submit a report, which includes you being hostile and belligerent, your status will be converted to inactive. That will be until they decide to conduct the needed tests to return you to active status at their convenience. Trust me when I say that you will be inactive for several weeks if not months. I know, because I've been there. Now nod to Agent Baker if you understand."

Leslie came back over the phone.

"I have no idea what you said, but she is being really nice to those guys now. Well, cooperative might be a better way of putting it. She still doesn't look happy."

I laughed, "She just got a bad bump on the noggin; she's not supposed to be happy. But, in any case, Jay and I have a couple of loose ends to tie up here; well, more to the point, we still have a mess to clean up over here, so we'll see you back at the office."

"I have one more," she said.

"You have one more what?"

"We had three locations to check out. This was number two, and the bad guys don't take a day off just because one of us has to go on sick leave."

"You just hold your horses there, you little 'go getter.' Not a good idea," I said.

"I thought you had faith in me."

"I do, but with everything going on, I have more faith in them. I wouldn't wanna go in there alone, so you're not going in there alone. Send me details and location; Jay and I will meet you there, so park it at a distance, and gather some intel until we get there."

"Yeah, yeah, sure," she said.

I worried that she might try something stupid from the cynical response; in any case, once I received the details, the fear that she might do something stupid subsided. We were between her and the last location on their list. We would be finished here and already there long before she would.

****

It took us an hour to get across town. I hadn't expected that much traffic at two in the afternoon. The worst part of it was it gave Deputy Director Peterson plenty of time to send me nagging requests for updates. I had only so many versions of 'I can't talk right now' and 'communication at this time could jeopardize personal safety.' She knew it was a smoke screen, of course; the last year of working together had pretty much exposed all my tricks. I used them anyway just to let them know I didn't give a squat.

We stopped about a block from our destination. From our vantage point, it was difficult to determine by eyeball the exact house, so we linked up the on-board computer with satellite surveillance. In the windshield, the house first outlined in red, and then the computer made a stepped incremental magnification until I told it to stop.

Too bad we didn't have the tech to see spectral images like the rollers could. Not that it would do us any good. Unless we could say that we had hard evidence that a crime was in progress, it was a violation of those people's invasion of privacy rights. For all we knew, the folks in this house were fine upstanding citizens who lived a clean, upstanding, taxpaying life.

"Car, I got a car coming down the street," Jay said.

I disengaged the lock on the house and used the touch screen of the windshield to select and follow the car.

"If I didn't know better, I'd say that looks like a PD undercover vehicle. They better not pull in that driveway."

They didn't; they drove past the house and then turned into the driveway of a house three houses down, on the opposite side of the street. We watched as they pulled into the garage.

"Well, at least we know that there's not an armored vehicle in that garage," he said.

"Shoot, for all we know this whole block was bought out by the FFB. Let's run a check on—"

The air pressure created by the roller that flew past caused the windows to rattle. Jay used some words I hadn't heard him say in a long time.

"What the hell?" She knew she wasn't supposed to approach the house alone. I was known for being bad at bending the rules, but I did know what lines not to cross.

When the vehicle came to a stop, the little head that popped up didn't belong to Leslie. It was Mercedes, and now I was boiling.

"Lord have mercy, somebody turn the burner down to simmer cause I'm about to blow. No way she has been medically cleared that fast."

"Oh, please," Jay said. "She doesn't have to listen to you. That's the Seattle Boss."

"Boss or not, she is still eligible to be kicked straight and directly in her ass."

Right after Mercedes removed herself from the vehicle, Leslie's head popped up. I guess recent events had started to catch up with Merce. While Leslie was in the process of unstrapping and disconnecting, Merce slowly walked around the roller and place it between her and the house.

Mercedes kept her eyes on the house, but as soon as she got out, Leslie looked down the street and threw us one of those big ole' grins.

Jay shook his head. "Dang, I can see those teeth from here. How much do you think a smile like that costs?"

"It would help if your father was a legend in nano-medical tech and lived in a big fancy house."

Jay shook his head. "I guess I'm stuck with this government-issued smile then."

It was then I notice the front door open up. I threw the car into drive, and I think we had them all covered within the first five steps he made out the door.

The person coming out held up a badge but was in plain clothes. When Jay and I stepped out of the car, each of us sporting a brand new MP 91c tactical submachine gun, he came to a stop and held up both hands.

"Whoa, take it easy, fellas. See?" He twisted his wrist and waved the badge like it would help us to see it better. "I'm one of the good guys."

Alonzo, followed by a uniform, came out of the house. "Dammit, Harris, you messing with my people again?" he asked.

"Crap, not you. I'm starting to think you're a stalker. Everywhere I go, you're there. Do I need to put a restraining order on you, Hernandez?"

"This is a homicide investigation. What are you doing here anyway?"

"This place has popped up on the watch list. I take it that this is a crime scene?"

"It is." He closed his eyes and gave a single nod.

"You mind if we come in and have a look?"

"I do." Again with a deep single nod. "The reason being, at the risk of contamination, we need to always minimize the number of personnel on the scene, and so far we haven't seen hide nor hair of a relic."

"Yeah, well, it sounds like I'm asking, but I'm just being cordial. Look at it this way, what we are looking for may help you with your Agrarian Mann murder investigation."

He stepped to the side and lifted an inviting hand—palm up—toward the door.

"Me and you, Merce," I said, and then leaned in toward her, with a whisper, "This is not over yet.

You, me, and that big lump on the side of your head need to have a serious discussion." I looked over to Jay and Leslie. "I suppose you two can sit this one out." I secured the MP snag in the vehicle and accessed the scene investigation kit.

After protecting our hands and going through the standard protect-the-crime-scene stuff, we started up the walkway. Alonso and the other plain clothes officer had already gone back in. The one uniformed remained outside.

We walked in, and it was the same old thing we had seen so many times before. Dead bodies—in this case two—were lying in the middle of the floor. Enough blood on the floor to fill a kiddie pool. The thing that bothered me the most was that it didn't bother me at all.

Alonzo was on the circuit, talking with who I had to assume was his boss and, as usual, chose to completely ignore us.

"Okay, Merce, this was on your list of hot spots, so this is your show. Where do we start?"

"Well, let's get out of their way for right now. We can work our way back to this room."

"No image set?" I asked.

"You know, you're right. This may or may not be an ARRU crime scene, but it is a crime scene."

"I'll call Jay," I said, "and let him and Leslie fight it out over who gets in-zees and who gets out-zees." She gave me a nod and started toward one of the bedrooms. I took out my phone, brought up the speed dial list, and called Jay.

"Hey, what's going on in there?" he asked. But, at the same time I got ready to answer, Mercedes stopped in the doorway and slowly turned around. I never believed in ghosts, but if they did exist, she was looking at one square in the eyeball.

"Hold on, let me get back to you," I said, and put away the device.

Mercedes walked back over to me and asked in a whisper, "What did he just say?"

"What, who— Jay? Jay was curious about—"

"You know what." She stepped back and started speaking normally. "We got better leads, and if this place was related, or had anything to do with relics, they would have come across them by now and called us. Let's get out of here." She turned back to Detective Hernandez. "Have you identified the victims yet?"

He muted the phone, "Not as of yet. It seem as though they have no criminal record."

"Thanks, Hernandez; please let us know what you find." She turned and started toward the front door.

I had to admit, I was a little perplexed. I turned to Hernandez and put my hands on my hips, "Yeah, what she said." It was the first time I could remember that he found any humor in my antics. He just laughed. I turned and followed Mercedes out.

"Hey you, wait up," I said. She had a good pace, and I didn't know if I would be able to catch her, so I broke into a jog.

"Sorry," she said. "I just need to get out of the yard."

When I finally caught up with her, she had made it to the roller and was ready to climb in.

"Whoa! Alright, you are going to have to let us in on the joke," I said. I grabbed her by the back of the arm. "Mercedes?"

"It's all wrong. Those people in there were just killed. The blood hasn't even started to coagulate yet." She looked back at the house and then shook her head. "Why aren't they wearing any gloves to protect the crime scene?" She paused and closed her eyes. "But, what got me the most is what he said on the phone. He said 'Ain't that a dingle-berry' to whoever he was talking to."

"Okay," Jay said. "You telling us you were spooked by a nerd? Who else would say something like that?"

It was then I notice Leslie had her mouth open and the same look on her face Mercedes had in the house. That was more than enough to give me a change of attitude.

I pulled out my snag and held it down by my thigh. I looked again and notice that Mercedes already had her snag out. You could barely see it. The only way I knew was that the bottom of the grip extended a half inch below the bottom of her fist. The rest of the weapon was hidden by her hand and the receiver was hidden behind her thigh.

I turned my attention to Jay to make sure we were all on the same page, but he was focused on the front door. He was fixed; his eyes were in a tight squint.

When I turned to see what was so important, Alonzo was standing in the doorway. He just stood there with his head tilted slightly and his eyes fixed on us. He stood there, feet shoulder width apart, and at a forty-five degree angle. I felt like a silhouette fifty meters down range, because the only thing missing was the weapon. He was definitely in a shooting pose. It was at that point we all knew.

"Salvo," Leslie whispered, but she didn't have to.

Hernandez made a slow walk backward, but the pose never changed. Eventually he disappeared into the darkness.

It was a one-grunt and a two-step process before Mercedes was back in the roller. I don't think I've ever seen her move that fast.

I heard the clicking of the connectors and cables used to make the communication between the rider and the vehicle, and then it started up.

"Welcome, Agent Molina," the roller's system said. "The high velocity ensemble is indicating an elevated heart rate."

"Merce, you wanna share your plan with us?" I asked. I heard the weapons on the vehicle load. "Hold on, Merce, slow it down. Take a breath, alright?"

I turned to Leslie. "When y'all rode up, I know y'all scanned the yard and driveway for traces of explosives. Right?"

She first nodded, and then replied, "Yeah, sure, definitely not going to make the same mistake twice."

"I'm fine, everything's good. Don't worry, I got your back if it heats up," came from the opening on the top of the roller.

Jay looked at the roller in confusion and then up at the sky. "Alright, let me get around back before you go in after him." He switched the safety off, and the ready light indicated that it was ready to fire.

"Under the circumstances, shouldn't we call for a MARRV?" Leslie asked.

I thought about it for a second. "We don't have that luxury. Besides, there's no protocol. We haven't seen any relics or recovery-related items. Anyway, by the time they got here, everyone would be long gone, including us if we just stand here out in the open." I looked back into the darkness of the doorway. "Waiting on you, Jay. Encryp-line 5." I got a nod, and then he started moving laterally to the house.

I turned to Leslie, "I got point; when we go in, I'll take five degrees right and everything left. You take five left and everything else. We go in fast and bold."

Mercedes's head popped up. "I'd feel better if you two were waiting in the car or on the other side of the roller until Jay got into position." Her head disappeared back into the vehicle again.

"Thanks, but we're okay, Merce. Tell you what, why don't you just hang out and make sure you watch our backs."

I was so focused on what would be coming out of that front door to get me that I forgot about the uniform standing next to the house. He hadn't moved, but he watched Jay while he moved the length of the house, and Jay was watching him. Since he was sweating and his left hand was trembling, I switched off my safety.

"Officer, I'm going to need for you to place your weapon on the ground and step back," I said. He looked into the doorway. "If you run, you won't make it. If you do anything other than what I'm telling you, you'll die."

He decided not to do what I was telling him.

His weapon was halfway out of the holster when the right side of his head exploded from the round that Jay put in his left temple. I continued to hold the sights over the officer even though he was down on the ground. I looked over at Jay.

"I had him," I said.

Jay just shrugged.

The gunshot was a clear announcement that we were coming. There was no more need for subtleties, so I bolted for the door.

As soon as I broke through the entryway, I moved left to give Leslie a chance to offset to my right. There was no one in sight. I kept scanning with my weapon, but I held up my left fist to let Leslie know to stop. I pointed to my ear and formed a cup around it to let her know to just listen. The eerie silence was broken by the sound of a collision.

I hated to do it, but I had to turn—maybe just a quick glance. I kept my weapon fixed on the interior of the house, but turned my head and shoulders to see what was going on outside. Instead of turning, Leslie came completely through the doorway, put her back against the wall, and continued to scan the interior.

On the street, the undercover vehicle we had seen earlier was speeding away, but all you could really hear was the sound of Mercedes screaming in her airborne flight across the front yard. There was an occasional pause in the screaming when the roller hit the ground and bounced back into the air. The third bounce didn't include a scream, but she did decide to share her feelings on the situation.

"This is BULL… SHIT…!"

The long trailing edge of the 'shit' finally ended when the roller slammed into the house next door. The vehicle became lodged in the cathedral window of what I guessed to be the dining room. If Leslie hadn't been looking directly at me, I would have been laughing my fool head off.

"I think we need to get the heck out of here," she said.

I took another quick look around, and because there was no one here and the places that these folks inhabited had a bad habit of blowing up, she was right.

We made it half way across the yard before we could see flames dancing on the inside of the windows.

"I could have sworn that you said the house was scanned for explosives."

Leslie shook her head. "I said we scanned the yard and driveway."

"Come on, they're getting away. Let's go." Jay looked like he was frustrated with me because my run had slowed to a walk.

"Jay, we can't leave Mercedes stuck in the wall like that; besides, we need to check and make sure everyone in the house is okay. There might be some injured civilians in there." He looked in Mercedes direction, turned back, and looked down the street at the escaping vehicle and then scratched his head.

"Hey Merce, you okay over there?" he asked.

"If you don't kindly walk your big ass over here and get me out of this wall, the only walking you're going to be doing is with a limp."

It was too much. Leslie and I both laughed, but the small explosion that caused the windows on the house to shatter reminded us of the seriousness of the situation.

"Get me out of here NOW!"

We started over in her direction. It was pretty obvious that Jay was irritated by the fact that Alonso had gotten away.

"Hey, where is he going to go?" I asked. "The man is a cop. The same mechanisms we use to protect the cops in the field nowadays will be the same tools that will make running for him impossible. He can only stay off the grid for so long."

A deep inhale and a hard exhale came from Leslie. "The question I have is how many others will be killed or injured before he turns up again?" We both stopped and looked at her.

"See, now that's what I'm talking about. You get 'em 'Wildcat.' Thank you… thank you," Jay said.

I looked at her and shook my head. "Why are you stirring up trouble? Haven't you learned you can't feed this man's ego?"

She shrugged. "I was just saying—"

"Shouldn't you be calling to make sure a fire control team is en route?" I said. She stopped and stood there while Jay and I continued toward Mercedes. She couldn't have possibly known the damage she had done. The house that was ablaze was nothing by comparison. Jay started right in on how we had the tiger by the tail and how we were only seconds from saving the world.

I knew I would have to listen to this all the way back to the office.

CHAPTER 15 – THE COLLECTION AGENCY

Some will watch you and some will emulate you; we all strive for greatness, so there should be no surprise that your achievements are idolized. As a Serendipitan, life is a leap for the stars. Don't allow lesser souls to hinder success by holding you back. Leap, reach, and command your star. Allow others to envy and idolize, it may be all they have. Book of Serendipitan Values, Chapter 7 (2077)

It was all so cloudy in my mind. I knew it would all eventually come to an end, but I was sure that by the time the end came, enough chaos would had befallen to make them all reconsider the whole concept of choking the life from the freedom of weapon of choice.

The sacrifices… the sacrifices I had made. They would all become pointless unless I could make them all see.

There was no point in becoming all misty-eyed now over the losses; nothing to do but push forward. I was a rogue warrior with no home. A Ronin is what I believe they called them.

The word on the details of how I had come into the leadership of the organization had spread like a pandemic throughout the FFB, and they wanted me more than the ARRU.

I had other connections, and I needed to bond with my new allies. If I was going to make—

"You alright there, Salvo?"

"What? Oh yes, just formulating… better yet, making minor adjustments to the plan."

"Oh yeah?" Steel said. "You want to let me in on it so I can plan the appropriate minor adjustments to the security measures?

I thought about it and figured it was time to cut my losses. "We're heading to East Texas—Tyler, to be exact. I know some people that can provide some leverage in my current situation. As for yourself? Once we get to Tyler, you're free to go. They can track me, but you're still a ghost. There's no need for the both of us to bite it."

I heard the sound of a handgun's receiver slam forward and looked over to see a 9 MM relic in his lap. He pulled out a cloth and polished the weapon.

"Well, let's stay flexible. You've already paid up until the end of the month."

I guess he had seen me trying to eyeball both the weapon and road; must have been the occasional swerve in the lane.

"Oh relax," he said before tucking the weapon away in a hip holster. "You—more than anyone else—should know that I'm a man of honor. When I take a job, I see it through till the end." Another weapon appeared. He removed the magazine and started cleaning the new weapon. "Of course, after the little covert stunt you pulled with the girl… what was her name again? Ah yes, CeCe; you do understand that at the end of the month I will make myself available for negotiations."

"Oh, of course." I had more than regret for Little CeCe; I had the feeling she, more than anything else, would somehow get her revenge, and Steel would probably help her out with that one.

He was right about one thing, though. I had plenty to worry about, but he wasn't one of them. Even way back on the Vanished Angels project, for this guy, his honor was more important than the paycheck. I always interpreted it as a way for him to save his soul and lessen the regret. He believed there was a special place for people of honor who do bad things. I tried to step on that dream several times, but he never allowed anyone to take it away from him.

Yeah, I had plenty to worry about. For starters, I had to get rid of the corpse in the trunk—and soon. If a State Trooper pulled us over, he would without a doubt use a sonic scanner to get a picture of what's in the trunk. That has been standard procedure since the VAP. If they found the dead owner of this vehicle, we would have to make dead troopers, and then the direction we're heading would be out of the bag.

****

It took two hours to get to our destination. Having to stop and get rid of the one hundred-ten pounds in the trunk slowed us down a bit, but we still made good time.

I had to get rid of everything Dallas PD issue. I wasn't exactly sure what all they could track. They tell you what they want you to know they track, but who's to say they tell you everything.

Topping the list was the media device; that one really sucked. I had set up a nice encrypted connection to my personal server on the thing, and the server had all my contact information in it. Yeah sure, everything that was FFB-related had a two-hundred and fifty-six bit encryption, secure behind a firewall, not to mention the signal I sent to wipe everything should have left nothing but a useless box, but those folks in forensics every so often come up with a miracle.

Sure, I took great care in disabling the power on the device and dropping it in a battery changer before making my way over to one of the safe houses. It was kind of tricky. Once you had the old battery removed, you still had to pull the power on the changer before it inserted a new battery. I had to be careful, because if I had made a mistake, it would have still told them where I had been, so that meant all the known safe houses were maybe not so safe.

I knew his vehicle. He was very predictable. It's one of the downsides of being an obsessive–compulsive. Everything has to be in a certain order.

The time was 3:45 PM. I expected him shortly after four. Since the pigmentation modifier would only work for several hours and then I wouldn't be able to use it again for twenty-four, I had to make sure to use the drug sparingly.

I still felt a little leery being out in the open; unfortunately, I had lost my means of setting up a secure meeting. There was nothing to do but wait.

He showed up, ten after four on the nose. It was hard to mistake him. It was hard to tell if the sunken in eyes were from the fact that he looked so malnourished or from a lack of sleep. Considering what I knew about his work habits, it was more likely from the latter.

Poor guy had no fashion sense whatsoever. His clothes were new, but the purple slacks and yellow shirt were not working for him. It made him look more like a clown than a professor. I couldn't accept it as a trade-off of being a genius because I was a pretty snazzy dresser myself.

I timed it so he and I could meet at his car at the same time. As soon as he got close enough, I got out of the car and headed straight for the vehicle. I heard the doors unlock.

"Hello, Professor Daniels; sorry to sneak up on you like this, but my options are a bit thin right now."

He looked at me with more curiosity than caution. "Have we met, Sir? The voice sounds familiar, but I'm having a little trouble placing the face."

"Well, it is our first face-to-face; but yeah, the voice should sound familiar since I have been your primary contact for some very hard to get items over the past year."

He tilted his head and slowly smiled. "Salvo? You know you really should take it easy with the pigmentation modifier. Studies have shown the long-term effects to become irreparable. You really could become a black man. Actually, a black man with a really bad skin condition."

Here I was out in the open, and he wanted to make small talk.

"It really is a nice day, but I think it might be better if we could discuss a few things in the car."

"Oh but of course." He leaned in, "Open passenger door."

The sound of the door unhinging was kind of comforting. I decided not to waste any time getting in, but he was really taking his time.

He threw his backpack and satchel onto the rear seat. When he started scrolling through his media device, my paranoia reached its peak. He almost fell backwards into the car when Steel grabbed his phone.

Steel made a quick scroll through his recent communications.

"Doctor Daniels, this is my associate… I guess you can call him Steel, or Mister Steel if you would like to be polite." Steel handed the device back to him, but the Professor acted like the darn thing had teeth when he took it back.

"Jeez, Mister Steel, you almost scared the crap out of me."

"Doctor, I need temporary asylum." We really needed to get down to business. "I have a couple of favors on the shelf with you and your group, and I'm going to need to call them in."

Steel came around to my side and tried the rear door.

"Would you mind?" I asked Daniels.

"What is this all about?

"It's like I said; it's about calling in a favor, and you really don't want us to get caught. If we get caught, that means you've been caught." The realization seemed to sink in.

"Open all doors," he said.

After all the doors were closed, Steel scanned for possible hidden communication devices. You had to look very closely to recognize the nod for the all-clear.

"Professor, I'm sure you're aware of my current situation, so I won't waste your time with the details. I need a place to lay low for a while. At least until me and my people can regroup and—"

"Salvo, I don't think there is any regrouping from where you've been." There was an element of sadness or perhaps pity in his voice. "You've been labeled a very bad, bad man; and, you've made the Federal Joint Task Force's Top Ten. But, you can only hope the Bureau or the ARRU find you before your own people. Lenard Anderson has put up half-a-million credits of his own money for your head. That, on top of what the Task Force is offering, makes you a tempting target."

I heard a deep breath and an exhale from the back seat. It kept coming back to me over and over. That unpleasant thought about the end of our agreement at the end of the month. Steel was a man of honor, but for him a contract was a contract, and there was no way I could continue to keep him financially content with my dwindling resources.

"Okay, so I don't have a lot of friends. But then again, I haven't ever really had; yet, I'm still here. Anyway, you and I still are. Right? We're still friends. Aren't we?" I had to brace myself for the lie.

"Of course. It's like you said: if you're caught, I'm caught, and that will just not do. You actually have it sort of easy by comparison. You just have to worry about getting shot. My associates are in search of test subject volunteers for experimentations. I've seen how some of the testing mistakes turn out, so I don't want to be on that list."

I shook my head, "And they say I'm a very bad man. You guys definitely raise the bar."

"Well, the Bureau doesn't have any idea about our plans." He held his chin up to indicate some sort of pride in their secret agenda.

"You mean, the Bureau doesn't have any idea about your plans YET." That was as direct and to the point as I could get.

"Alright, I have a cabin in a remote location where you can take respite."

"Take what?"

He smiled. "A pause, a break in your normal activities."

"Now that sounds like something I could use. A respite. Shall we go now?"

"Sure, I just need to swing by the house and get the key. I would imagine you're going to need some supplies as well."

The rear car door opened at the same time he started the car. Steel headed back toward the stolen car we came in. "Are you sure we can trust him? The mercenaries we been working with are an unsavory group of characters."

"Undying… undying trust. Well, at least until the end of the month. He is only going to get the car; we can't very well leave it here. We have genetics all over it, and it would sit much prettier in a remote location.

It took us about twenty minutes to get to his home. I was feeling pretty secure, until he pulled into the garage and closed the door behind us. I pulled my weapon from the holster and discovered that the tight fit in the garage wouldn't let me open the door. Without Steel, it felt like I was missing a leg. I gently caressed the trigger.

"Sorry about the door," he said. "If you don't mind, could you slide over and get out on this side?"

"Whether I mind or not, it's not like I have a choice." I slid out and started to make note of any and all possible escape routes. Half of the garage was littered with an assortment of what was obviously chemical test equipment. I had to bend and twist in all kinds of directions to make my way to the house door.

"You're safe here. Do you think you really need that thing?" he asked.

I looked at him for a moment and then resumed my observation of the maze that supposedly led to the house door. "As you are aware, I'm a pacifist, and typically I wouldn't allow one of those in my house; however, considering the circumstances—well, come on in."

I followed him through what appeared to be a laundry room that had been transformed into a laboratory.

I walked silently as I could while I listened to every creak, every click that floated within earshot. Where was Steel? We made our way to the living room, and the only word that came to mind was pigsty. Considering all the stuff I had to step over in the garage to get in here, I pretty much expected it.

"You can wait right here," he said. "I'll retrieve the key, and we'll be on our way."

I had no choice but to trust him. Once I was in the cabin—if he wanted to turn me in—they would come in the night like a winter wind. I couldn't kill him. The ARRU and Bureau probably wouldn't make the connection when his body turned up, but his people would. This whole area would be swarming with relic-packing contractors, and where relics go, the ARRU follows.

The best course of action would be to set up a lookout point half-a-klick from the cabin and watch it for a couple of days. We'll need some thermal blankets in case a hovercraft begins to search—

The sound came from the kitchen area. The broken silhouette of the shadow moved from left to right on the living room floor.

Decent cover was hard to find in the room I was in. The chair I had chosen would only conceal my location until I got a shot off. After that I was a goner.

"Is that you, Salvo?"

I stood and dropped the weapon to my side and held it against my thigh. "Thanks, Steel, for a second there, I thought I was scared, and it has been a long time since I felt real fear. For a second there, I thought—"

He slowly entered the room, scanning with his weapon from top down. His eyes shifted from left to right, and the barrel of the relic class, semi-auto MP5 moved from right to left.

In a low tactical stance he made his way across the room. I raised my weapons to the ready and kept talking so not to arouse suspicion if whoever he was looking for was listening.

"For a second there, I thought you were one of the bad guys. At least, from my point of view."

He made his way over to me and whispered. "The lock on the back door was busted."

"Found it!" Daniels had no idea what he would be walking back into. He went looking for a key, but what he found when he came back were the barrels of a 9MM and a MP5 pointed at each of his eyeballs.

"See," he said. "This is one example and why I typically don't allow those things in my house."

"Were you aware that the lock on your backdoor is broken?" I asked. The surprised look on his face said it all for him. He wasn't.

"Why don't you just come over here and have a seat on the couch," Steel said and pointed with his weapon in the direction of the sofa. He turned to me. "I'm going to make a quick sweep. Be right back." He disappeared into the main hallway. I found the center of a non-street side wall and squatted down with my back against it.

The professor leaned back and crossed his legs. "You guys are a bit over the edge; don't you think?"

I looked at him and smiled. If he knew what type of life I had really led, it would be much clearer.

He cleared his throat and shook his head before continuing. "I would imagine that it would be exhausting living your life like this. How long do you think you will be able to keep this up?"

"As long as it is, or as long as there is no more need to," I said.

Steel came back with his weapons lowered and was much more relaxed.

I felt a weight lift off my chest.

"No one is here, but there isn't any dust on the catwalk in the attic. Our friend here doesn't appear to have an obsession with cleaning, so I'm going to guess someone cleaned up their footprints."

"Bomb?" I asked.

"More likely surveillance; I think someone's listening." The words Steel whispered brought back that uneasy feeling. He removed a fist-sized cylinder from his belt and unscrewed it until it became two pieces.

"What do you have there?"

"Oh, one of the newer products from the iSpy corporation. It's called a Mini-mobile Aerial Camera or MACAM for short. I call it peace of mind."

He squeezed the one in his right hand and twin rotors popped out of the top. An eyepiece popped out the other. He walked over near the window and spoke into the eyepiece like it was a microphone.

"Altitude – one hundred feet."

The blade spun-up and started screaming. They were moving so fast you couldn't even see them. The way he threw it, it looked like he slung a curve ball, but it went straight through the window.

"What the—you couldn't open the window first?" Daniels was on his feet and appeared to be very upset.

"Sorry," Steel said. "That's what it said to do in the instructions."

Daniels looked at me like I was supposed to scold him.

"When you don't follow instructions, that's when people get hurt," I said.

The way his lips tightened up said he didn't like my response.

Steel didn't care; he stood there with the eyepiece pressed against his face, occasionally sliding his thumb like he was guiding the—'macam' is what I believed he called it.

"This is so cool," he said. "Lots of cars on the street. Looks like three of them have people inside. I'll have to go check 'em out before we hit the road."

He walked over to the window, raised it, and then placed his back against the wall. I had to guess the eyepiece acted like a homing beacon because he gave the command, "End search, return home." He positioned the eyepiece in front of the open window and waited. A few seconds later, we heard the screaming of the rotors getting louder and louder. The crash from the window on the opposite wall made all of us dive for the floor. The aerial device came bouncing into the living room.

"Dammit, dammit, and for the last time dammit!" The professor lowered his head, and then placed the bridge of his nose between his thumb and index finger.

Steel picked up the camera piece, retracted the blades, and started reassembling the thing. He used a knife-hand to point in the direction of the three vehicles. I noticed him counting under his breath between each one.

"You mind if I use your gentleman's room?" he said to the professor.

"Sure, why not. While you're in there, why don't you kick a few holes in the walls?"

Steel turned toward me. "I shouldn't be no more than ten minutes. If it's more than that, I'm having a little trouble, so bring the laxatives."

I knew what he meant. "Yeah right, extra strength." He disappeared out the broken back door.

I wasn't so used to placing so much faith in anyone on this level. This relationship with Steel made me a bit nervous. Yeah, I could put my faith in a contractor, but he had the option to team up with the relics out there for a heck of a payday. Felt like the walls were closing in, and eventually I would have to start shooting in all directions.

Five minutes passed, and then ten.

"Alright, Professor, I think it's time we make a break for it."

"What about your friend?" he asked.

My friend. Steel was probably the closest thing I had to that word, but it wasn't the case.

"He's a big boy and knows how to take care of himself very well, so let's go."

"Wait… wait!" He stood up and turned his ear toward the front of the house.

I heard tires, and then I saw the shadow of the car move across the window curtain. I pressed my back against the wall next to the window and took a quick peek.

There were two cars, parked bumper-to-bumper like a barricade. Four of the unsavory kind got out, and they all moved to the opposite side of the vehicles.

"What is it?" The professor had a look of terror on his face.

"It's the collection agency," I said.

Daniel's phone rang. He jumped and then grabbed his heart. "Crap, I'm too old for this. Hello?" There was a short pause before he stretched out his arm. "It's for you."

I returned to the window and considered my options.

He finally walked over and offered me the phone; obviously, it was important to him that I took the call.

I put the phone to my ear but didn't have to say anything. I knew they were watching.

"Salvo, the Local Law Enforcement is currently on a wild goose chase, but unfortunately for you, the bank robbery they are investigating is on the far end of the county. No one is coming to rescue you.

"In any case, I'm sure the neighbors see us out here packing steel and are right now making the appropriate phone calls. Since I'm not one for taking chances, I would like to get out of here in the next two minutes just in case Sheriff Billy Bob—or whoever—makes the connection and drops the investigation of the alarm.

"You have one minute to come out. If we don't see your happy face in one minute, it will take us 1.5 minutes to drag your body out and we will still be on our way in two. You have fifty-two seconds remaining."

This was it, there was no back door I could make a break for. There were no trap doors underneath the bar that would allow me to make an escape. I knew what to expect from the beginning. For me, I knew I would either become the Deliverer or have to embrace death. Alright, this was it. If I had to go, I was going to go like Agrarian. It was going to be a fight and they would have to look me in the eye; they would know that there was no fear.

"Salvo, what did they say?" The professor's voice started to sound like nagging.

I looked back outside, only to see two of the contractors holding handheld rocket launchers.

"Get down!" I dived behind the couch, but Daniels just stood there dumbfounded.

The pressure from the explosion pushed me and the sofa across the room and pinned me against the wall. There was only sheetrock and insulation where Daniels had been standing.

I looked around the end of the couch and saw four heads rising over the rubble. They were coming in fast and all carried handguns.

It seemed silly to be thankful that four highly trained killers were approaching with handguns, but I was. It kind of evened the playing field. They had pistols and so did I. I knew I wouldn't make it, but I probably could get at least two of them.

I knew they were close. I could hear the sounds of what was left of the front of the house crackling underneath their feet.

I had to move quickly; I would move faster than the eye could follow. Pop up, hit two, drop-roll, and take out the others. What a crappy plan.

When I popped up, before I could get a shot off, the entire lower jaw of the man on the left exploded. It was the distraction I desperately needed. I hit the guy just to his left, square in the chest, before I was spun to the right by the round that tore through my right shoulder. I fell behind the couch and quickly made my way to the opposite end. There it would be easier to use my left as primary shooting hand.

I scooted and angled around the couch to get a good shot. I discovered Steel and the remaining two in a firefight. Steel had taken up position behind the two vehicles, and from my vantage point it looked like they were caught between the two of us. I had often heard people whisper when I had my back turned that if I ever got any advantage, I would ride it and exploit it to the ends of the earth. I needed that to be true now more than ever.

Steel had the protection of the vehicles, but they had knocked down the wall of the front of the house. There really wasn't any place for them to take cover except behind the pile of rubble they had created.

The one on the right tried to slither off for better cover. A real badass I guess, 'cause he had his body pressed as flat as possible on the ground. He dragged everything, including his face, through the broken glass and fragments of what remained of the house.

My shot hit him in the thigh. It was enough to cause him to go on the offensive. He had to roll to get a better shot at me, but it's when he lifted his head the round I sent him found his nasal cavity. I'm going to say damned lucky shot from the left side.

"Hold your fire!"

The shout came from the center of the rubble, and then a handgun flew out. Smart move; he really had no other option.

The sheetrock started to move over on my right. Since Steel had the remaining gunner covered, I made my way over to the moaning to find a battered and beaten Daniels.

I helped him up but couldn't really tell whether he was more in shock from the explosion or the new view of the street from his house.

"Well, pack my ass with bananas and coconuts," he said, while dusting himself off. "Look at my house. My house, my house; they weren't suppose… they didn't have to—"

"They weren't supposed? Go ahead and finish it, Professor; they weren't supposed to what?"

He looked at me like I had some nerve to read between the lines. "I'm standing in what used to be my coat closet, and you look at me like I would sell us both down the river."

I turned away and headed over to Steel and the survivor.

"Hey, Salvo." He smiled like we were old friends. "You know this is not personal. I was just telling Steel here how we were supposed to take you alive."

I looked at Steel. "You two know each other?"

"We have history," he said.

"Oh yeah?" I look back down at the gunman, on his knees, with his fingers interlaced behind his head. "I figured they would all want me dead. Who wants me alive?"

He turned his head and looked up at me. "Everyone. You name the organization. The FFB, the

Bureau, the ARRU. Hell, I think we could sell you to Mothers Against Adrenaline Drivers."

"Yeah, but who hired you?"

A pause of silence filled the air.

"Can't say for sure." He looked over at the man I had just killed. "You've killed the man that handled the negotiations, but you should thank us. We have already taken out the two groups that beat us here. They weren't as nice as us, but we were better."

"Then you're no good to me." I raised my snag and pointed between his eyes. He rolled his face upward and closed his eyes.

Steel's weapons dropped between the tip of my barrel and his face. "There's really no need to do that," Steel said.

Taking him out was already part of my plan," I said. "This man is a threat."

He shook his head, "No, this whole area is a threat, and since I'm in charge of security, I say we move on."

I felt to let him go would be the same as shooting myself in the head. "It's a bad decision. If we let him live—"

"If you do it, I would have to consider our contract null and void. Right now, you're as safe as you possibly could be." He pushed my weapons away with his and continued, "Until the end of the month."

It couldn't be any clearer than that. Darkness was closing in from all sides, and Steel was telling me that I only had five days left of freedom.

The look in his eyes said that if I were to shoot him, I wouldn't get off a second shot. Steel was the closest thing I had to a friend, and in five days… in five days it would be all over. He had said it before. He had told it to me over and over, but I only heard what I wanted to hear. The truth was: in five days I would be out of friends, and the only place left for me to hide would be the RV that Steel and I had stashed several weeks ago.

With this relationship Steel and I had crumbling the way it was, I couldn't consider the RV a safe house any longer. Well, unless Steel was out of the picture.

CHAPTER 16 – MOMENTS

I have no words to offer that would provide the same level of comfort that the parents would feel if they held a relic in hand once they found the perpetrator or perpetrators. First and only Media Circuit interview of noted Relics Rights Advocate, Daniel Sharp, when asked: "What do you say to the parents of the children slain by relics?"

It had been four days… four whole days since we lost track of Alonso. I was sure that he would've turned up by now, but up until now the only things that turned up were bodies—bodies of contractors and civilians alike.

I hated to say it, but Jay and Leslie were right. We had let him get away, only to leave a trail of death and destruction in his wake. Several people missing between here and Tyler, but I'm not going to dwell on the whole mess down there. I still have my hands full with the cleanup of the Reverend Tomkins fiasco.

I'm sure most were false leads, but there were sightings as far east as Mobile and as far north as Kansas City.

I knew he would get tired of running, but the phone call this morning had come as a complete surprise.

"I want to make a deal," he had so eloquently put it. What in the hell made him think anyone was going to cut him a deal?

He knew all the lines, but I fed them to him anyway. "I'll talk to the DA, but really it all depends on what you can give us," I told him.

He started laughing at the bullshit, and so did I. Finally, he said. "I guarantee you, what I have… for what I'm offering, they should set me up in a cottage in Brazil." The only real question going through my mind was how this guy could still be alive.

The directions were very specific: park in the Blue honeycomb garage, above the 'E' level. Figured it would have to be a half mile walk from the mall entrance. I guess he wanted to watch me walk alone to where we were supposed to meet.

There was a media device vendor on the second floor. I was supposed to ask for Daphne. I guess a vendor name would have helped because there were four on the second floor alone.

I went to each one in turn, and, as fate would have it, the last vendor had a Daphne.

When I asked if she had anything for me, she looked around and then whispered, "Are you Special Agent Harris?" Being the fun-loving, good natured guy that I am, I looked around and whispered back,

"Yeah," and then pressed my index finger to my lips. "But don't tell anybody."

She slid and envelope over to me and then went to the other side of the counter to help another customer. Funny, funny stuff.

I tore open the envelope and pulled out the phone, which immediately started ringing.

"Hey Daphne, I'm guessing you configured this phone and no one else ever had possession of it?"

"That's correct sir. Is there anything wrong?"

I shook my head and waved her off. I turned around and walked away, feeling pretty sure it wasn't going to blow my head off.

"Hello, Alonso. I thought this was a face-to-face."

"The actual face-to-face is dependent on the outcome of the negotiations," he said.

"Oh yeah?" I looked over the railing, and although there were many people using their media devices, there was one that stood out. "Hold on, I'll be right down."

He was sitting next to a fountain, so I pitched the phone into the water to let him know I knew where he was. He was the only one that didn't jump or duck. He just looked up at me and squinted.

Seemed like he had it all figured out. It was a long trek around to even be able to access the lower level from where I was. I supposed that was just in case he needed an out and had to run. I knew he wasn't about to run, though. If he wanted to keep running, he wouldn't have called me or been here.

The question I had was: Would he stay put until I got there?

I had to admit I was pretty antsy. There were some mixed feelings because even though I was curious about what he had to say, I also knew I didn't care.

I approached the fountain, and he was still there. I'm going to say he was still there because he was a man that had run out of options. He had to be to call me.

"If it isn't the infamous Salvo. I have to admit, you make for a pretty cute little old black lady. You do know that stuff is damned brutal on a liver right? I hear the stomach and bowels get in a bad way when you start to revert back to your natural skin color. Is that true?"

I saw a hint of a smile at the corner of his mouth.

"Yes, well, I have a medical cannabis prescription," he said, "and after a brownie or two it all goes away."

I just nodded. "So how long do you plan to keep this up? This running thing."

He started to look around.

"No one is coming. I said I would come alone, and I did."

He turned to me and the intensity of his new life showed in his eyes. "I hope so. I'd hate for that daughter of yours to become an orphan. There is a sniper ready to blow a hole in your chest."

I shrugged, turned, and sat down next to him. "Yes, well, you and I, it seems we've lived most of our lives with that bulls eye between our eyes; or in this case, on the chest. Haven't we?"

He closed his eyes and fell into some type of quiet meditation.

"Sniper, huh? I thought you were all out of friends."

"I have one—sort of," he said. He opened his eyes and finally looked me in the eyes. "For one more day," he said.

I shook my head in disbelief. How could I be here… here, right now, holding a casual conversation with the most wanted man in the country?

"Alonso, I just have to ask; No, I need to know. Why this? Why all of this? You… this connection to the FFB; why this war on The Gun Control Act?"

He looked at me, and even though I was unclear about a lot of things, when I looked into his eyes I was sure about his resolve to rid the world of snags, or at least the current restrictions on relics.

"Moments," he said.

"Moments?"

"Yes, it's all about moments… moments in time. You see, every one… every single person will have a moment when they will need a relic," he said. "Mine came at the age of thirteen. That's when I stole my sick uncle's revolver and shot him in the chest." He paused, as if remembering. "He didn't die immediately, but all the begging and pleading that followed fell on deaf ears. Why should his pleas be heard? From the age of six to eleven, all the begging and pleading I did weren't heard. I think the more I cried, the more pain he inflicted, the more he enjoyed it. I still remember the breath reeking of alcohol. Occasionally he used ropes, but most of the time he took a lot of pleasure simply holding me in place by my hair. I knew… I knew one day there would be a moment. When my moment came, I needed a relic. One day, you, too, will have a moment when you need that relic. Everyone does… everyone at some moment in their life will need a relic."

I gave another nod. "My moment has come and gone. It was when I saw you back at the house, standing in the doorway. So what is it you think I can do for you, Alonso? My part in this is all but over. The FFB and the relic-running part of the organization have been completely dismantled—with your help, thank you. Hell, we have people stepping on other people to turn themselves in just to make sure that we know that they have no affiliation with you and your shenanigans whatsoever."

Alonso nodded in agreement and began to pour out his soul. "You may not believe this, but I have a lot of respect for you, your team, what you do, and how you do it. There are few people I would trust and so should you; however, I do trust you. You're so much on the up-and-up that it makes me want to puke sometimes and yes, I trust you. All these things are just scratching the surface. The Governor's Coalition, the FFB, Bar None… everybody has got their sticky fingers in the pie, and it's all related. What you don't know is that there are two more very dangerous groups out there and they scare the living hell out of me. I need your help. I need your help to stop them, and they MUST be stopped."

I saw the terror in his eyes. None of it made any sense. "Why do you care?" I asked. "You're getting ready to rot away in prison."

He shook his head. "I know too much. I'm getting ready to die in a prison. I give it three days at best, but if I were assisting you with your investigation, I would instantly have the protection of five bad-ass ARRU agents. You need my help, Harris. You see, I've been working both ends, and on one side I can point out police officers, city officials, doctors, as well as the people on the street. On the other end, I can give you names of judges, politicians, and the like. Regarding the two groups I just mentioned, one of them is a group of scientists that I've been providing a sort of a laundering service to for some very hard to get items. What I didn't know, and what I recently discovered, is that they have an agenda far more radical than I could've possibly imagined. It's all up to you. I can give them to you; I can give them all to you. Or, you can hand me over and give me to them."

I looked at him and I heard him, but all I saw was the most vile, evil thing since mama evil gave birth to sloth. I imagined a man covered in sores and boils. I could picture him in many ways, but I couldn't picture me working with him.

I stood up, closed my eyes, and listened to the sound of the water dancing on the fountain. I was in a calm place again. I started to walk away. "You should turn yourself in, Salvo."

About ten steps into my exit, he decided to make a final pass.

"Did you know I used to be a contractor? I was a young man, no identity, no records. With the right connections, it was easy for me to be put in the system. Go to the Police Academy and start a new life. Why'd I do it? Because I wanted to make a difference; I wanted to be part of something… something good for a change. I say this, and you wonder how I could've done the things I have recently. Well, some of us are haunted by ghosts. I have done things during the Vanished Angels Project that make recent events seem like playtime.

"Compared to what I did during the Project, this thing that's coming down the pike will seem like Armageddon. How will you feel when you see the world burning, and you come to realize that you could have done something about it?"

Could I just walk away from this? I had just told myself that Jay and Leslie were right, and if I were to let Salvo loose on the streets again, I guess you could say that the next death would be on me.

I closed my eyes again and swallowed back down the bile trying to escape from my stomach. I turned around, but just couldn't say it. Thank God it was in my eyes.

"Good!" he said. What sure looked like a sweet little old black lady stood up and took off her wig like she was getting ready for a fight. "Let's get ready for war."

END BOOK TWO

ABOUT THE AUTHOR

RIVAL TERRITORY is the second novel of Dale Jefferies and Book Two in The Relic Recovery Series. Twenty years in the Navy has helped shape his world view, knowledge, and culture. Thirty years in technology has challenged and stimulated his imagination. He and his wife currently reside in Arlington, TX.

www.ingramcontent.com/pod-product-compliance
Lightning Source LLC
Chambersburg PA
CBHW070606130626
46556CB00001B/290